Helen Mathers

A Man of Today

A Novel: Vol.III.

Helen Mathers

A Man of Today
A Novel: Vol.III.

ISBN/EAN: 9783337043537

Printed in Europe, USA, Canada, Australia, Japan

Cover: Foto ©Andreas Hilbeck / pixelio.de

More available books at **www.hansebooks.com**

A MAN OF TO-DAY.

A Novel.

BY

HELEN MATHERS,

AUTHOR OF

"COMIN' THRO' THE RYE," "SAM'S SWEETHEART,"
"MY LADY GREEN SLEEVES," "CHERRY RIPE!"
"STORY OF A SIN," ETC., ETC.

"What will you have?" quoth God.
"Pay for it and take it."

IN THREE VOLUMES.

VOL. III.

LONDON:

F. V. WHITE & Co.,
14, BEDFORD STREET, STRAND, W.C.
1894.

PRINTED BY
KELLY AND CO. LIMITED, 182, 183 AND 184, HIGH HOLBORN, W.C.
AND MIDDLE MILL, KINGSTON-ON-THAMES.

TO THE MEMORY OF

My Dear and Honored Friend

MORELL MACKENZIE.

CONTENTS.

BOOK II.—THE BITE.

[CONTINUED.]

BOOK III.—THE PUNISHMENT.

Book ii.—The Bite.

[CONTINUED.]

CHAPTER XIII.

" All the bodies of the universe are allied by sympathies
or natural antipathies."

—AGRIPPA DI NETTESHEIM.

HAVE you ever kneeled down to look in a
dog's eyes, when first he comes, a stranger, to
your house? Wistful, earnest, they will
search yours, probing your very soul to see
what you really are, what your meaning towards him is, and kneel there as long as you
will, that vigilant question will not relax, and
only by his after-conduct will you be able to
tell if you have answered to his enquiry satis-

factorily, though, if you pass with honours, you may safely be trusted in every relation of life.

Hugon met some such look from Nan as she turned her fierce gaze upon the child, and gradually it wavered before those earnest eyes, so full of pity, of comprehension, and of love.

"Poor soul," said Nan, putting her arms round the frail figure, "you have been very ill, but you will be better soon," and she kissed her gently on the cheek.

The warm human touch for the moment pierced the woman's despair, she looked up at the child, then pointed to the clothes scattered all round her on the floor.

"I tried to put them on," she said, "to run away, only I'm too weak. They all slipped through my fingers, but I shall get off all the same. The old ladies won't take me back, but there is one way out of every difficulty"—she stopped abruptly, and a sense of the wrong she was doing this young soul silenced her.

" You are only a bit of a child," she said, " and you and I never quite hit it—good and bad people seldom do."

" You are not bad," said Nan stoutly.

" I am not a good woman," said Hugon. " I can't see the one path ruled straight up to Heaven, and the other ruled straight down to hell. There are so many roundabout ways, trending up and down, and sometimes the path that seemed to lead upwards leads you quite the other way. It is like our virtues that are mostly restrained vices—even as our vices are virtues gone mad from repression—but I am forgetting again that you are only a child."

" Yes, but I understand," said Nan earnestly. She knew that Jem was at the bottom of the trouble, though he was in no way to blame for it, and she could follow the working of Hugon's mind easily, and honored the instinct that made flight appear Hugon's

3½*

one chance of salvation. There came an interruption in shape of a knocking, and the sound of Jem's cheery voice on the other side of the door.

"Nan," he called out, "you are in there, I know, and you've got to dress Hugon, and make her come down—I'll carry her—and Mr. Denison says if she don't, he'll fetch her, bed and all—so hurry up! Now, Hugon, I hope you are listening, because both he and I are in earnest—" and then he laughed, and went whistling away.

For awhile Hugon sat without moving, then, "Help me, Nan," she said.

When Jem came back half an hour later, following with all the coolness of a married man close on his knock, he just strode over to Hugon, picked her up like a baby, then in the middle of the room stopped still to look down at the wan face pillowed on his shoulder.

"Poor little girl," he said, thinking remorsefully of how he had grudged Easter's time to her, and his many grumblings, " poor, poor little woman ! "

He who had so much—Easter—everything —had grudged this poor waif a few days' shelter beneath his roof, and at the thought, his face softened with that tenderness which only strong men can know or feel.

And she looked up at him, alas! as a flower stretches towards the sun, and if God had taken her that minute, it would have been well, for she would have gone out into the darkness warmed through and through by a love wrought to its highest manifestation of good, and having fought the brave fight, and done Jem no harm, would have been reverently remembered by him all his life through.

But in place of Death was Life—greedy, entreating, crying out for what was not, nor ever could be its own, and Nan was the only one of them all who comprehended, or saw anything.

CHAPTER XIV.

"Sorrow may endure for a night, but joy cometh in the morning."

AFTER the night, morning : from the stress and fury of a storm-beaten darkness with its keening wail, its moan of drowning mariners upon the sea shore, lo! to the azure, and glory, and rain-washed breezes of the dawn, ay, and that exceeding joy which once promised alike to saint and sinner, has never failed us through all the ages since the promise was first given.

And even as Nature is in big, so is human nature in little, and we may mourn and suffer as we will through our dark hours, but the eternal freshness of hope, the pure love of life will assert itself at the first break of day in our hearts, and we are up and away, longing to take our share, to play our little part in that vast arena, where there is room and to spare for one and all of us to be happy, as God intended all his human families should be.

And Jem, lulled in the usual security of the unawakened married man, and seeing Easter brighter than she had for a long while been, did not always insist on accompanying her when she ordered out that dog cart which seemed to afford her so much pleasure, and attended by a groom only, sent Rufus flying over the miles that lay between Penroses and the Shaw.

There must have been wild blood surely in Easter's veins, so intense was the longing occasionally upon her to run away from the elegant order of her home, and disport herself like a wanderer on the world's face, and she had not left school so long, but that to her liberty was sweet, and even as she loathed the barouche and grey horses in which she and Jem returned duty calls on dull neighbours, did she love these harum scarum drives, and the feeling of independence that they always brought her.

Maria was not just then at home, as the two last babies had been indisposed, and on being removed to the sea-side, with most of the Shavers, had promptly developed measles, so that there was a sort of quarantine between the elder and the younger portion of the family, and Easter fell so easily into her old place that sometimes she tricked herself into believing that she had never run away to be married, or indeed got married at all!

These cheerful voices, that noisy school-room filled a want in her heart she had not hitherto acknowledged, but she had come to know that there is no loneliness like that of a married girl who has been one of an over-flowingly large family, and sometimes she did not want to go back to the Shaw at all, and often wished that no wedding ring had ever marked her finger.

For wherever she moved, Basil moved also, and she seemed to see him in every nook and corner of the garden, where she had so often seen, and regarded him not. *Now*, a herb or flower, or tree, would flash some memory upon her of how he had looked, of what he had said, when she had not seemed to listen, and beneath the trees in the orchard she would stand still with beating heart, listening so intently that at last she could almost *feel* his footsteps coming towards her, though no blade of grass bent beneath them, and no whisper of the wind uttered her name. Had he loved her then ? Did he love her now ?—ever wish that in spite of Daddy Gardner he had taken her in his arms that moonlight night, whether she would or no, and kissed her ?

He was Basil, and all was said. Just as he had once chosen to withhold himself from her, so in Town he had chosen to reveal himself, making other men but poor creatures beside him, and indeed it had been characteristically remarked that though men often boasted of being taken for him, no one was ever known to mistake Basil Strokoff for any other man whatsoever.

Tom Denison was not communicative to his daughter on the subject of the young Russian, what had been done was a matter of business between the two as men, and he did not wish it alluded to. It did not occur to him that Nan, who was growing up with great rapidity under her experiences, was the originator of this conspiracy of silence, and that Dinkie and the Snapper had several times choked off the most innocent remarks, because they happened to include the name of Basil. What reasons Nan had given, or how she contrived to muzzle those slippery tongues, it would be hard to say, but it is a fact that a whole fortnight elapsed before Easter found out how, but for merest chance, she and Basil must have met more than once lately, and it came about by accident, as such things mostly do. She was roaming through Penroses one day when she happened to enter the Blue room, which a housemaid was just then putting straight, and she asked in surprise who had occupied it.

" Prince Strokoff, ma'am," said the girl, astonished at Mrs. Burghersh's ignorance.

A wave of wrath swept over Easter, wiping out that intimate personal feeling of his near presence that had dizzied her. How *dared* they . . . and what were they afraid of—of him or of her? And what was *he* afraid of, to acquiesce in this insolent conspiracy of deceit?

There were, as Dinkie vulgarly put it, " ructions " in the schoolroom shortly afterwards, and Nan's sensations were the usual ones of the person who intermeddleth with a fool and his folly—only to confirm that fool in the same.

Henceforth Easter asked no questions, and came more seldom, but a restless fever

possessed and tormented her, and she began
to have a feeling that Basil had turned into a
shadow that for ever mocked and evaded
her. She seemed to see him fleeing out of
one door, as she entered by another—to hear
the sound of his steps echoing in Penroses the
moment she had passed beyond actual earshot
of them, and she anxiously searched the
innocent pink and white faces of her brethren
for a knowledge of this guilty passion of hers,
the danger of which a mere child like Nan
had been able to discover.

Meanwhile Jem was making Hugon happy,
and probably no man is insensible to the
charm of conferring intense happiness on
someone else, the more especially if that
someone has known little or no pleasure in
her life, and Jem enjoyed showing her the
pictures, the prints, the many treasures of an
old house that had been enriched by the
taste of generations of cultured people, not
knowing that Hugon's supreme content was

in him—and not in those things upon which he discoursed to her.

She could bear even to hear him talk of Easter, since the voice was his. She could bear anything so long as she had so large a share of his time — his company, and resolutely she put the future aside, and, since every dog has his day, this day being hers — she, as the dog, enjoyed it to the uttermost.

And it is a subtle distinction, but a true one, that a woman often finds an excuse for her unlawful love of a man, in the fact that his wife does not love him too much, or indeed at all. And Hugon knew that the hour had struck when any true friend of Easter's would have seized her with a strong hand, and in very despite of herself, dragged her back from the precipice on which she stood, and the one person who could have opened Jem's eyes—who could urgently have cried to him, "Take her away—take her out of herself—

remove her from everything that can remind her of Basil, every chance of seeing him," was silent, and in this crowning temptation of her life—fell.

None had interposed to save *her* in her darkest hour—no angel from Heaven—no voice from earth had come to stay *her* hand in its gloomy deed, that yet was the supreme rejection by the spiritual self of its baser one, and was she the keeper of Easter's soul, or was that wanton soul even worth the keeping? Jealous love may in time become hurtful as envy, that "daughter of pride," "the author of murder and revenge—the beginner of secret sedition . . . the filthy slime of the soul. A venom, a poison — a quicksilver" . . . and had not some such quicksilver run in Hugon's veins ever since that moment of unreason, in which she had barely restrained herself from tearing Easter as an interloper out of Jem's arms?

"Why don't you go up to Town for the

season ? " said Hugon one day, when they sat together in the White Pavilion.

" O, you *know*—Jem's uncle is dying, and Jem's his heir, he may have to go off to Scotland at any moment, and how am I to frivol around, in the midst of Jem's relations too, in black ? "

" You always wear black ? "

" Yes, but not weepers. And Jem's quite happy," added Easter, "and when a man's happy he won't stir. He only travels when he's wretched."

" *My* travels must begin soon," said Hugon, grimly conscious that however evil her desires, the Devil showed no present signs of enabling her to gratify them.

Easter looked concerned. Formerly, she had not pitied Hugon very greatly, being herself serene, with the selfish serenity of perfect health. It is when we are nervous, trembling to each suggestion of pity, of kindness, that we feel for others, because we feel for them through ourselves, but when we are well and happy, our nerves are of steel, and our sympathies are calloused through and through.

We carry this selfishness into our every relation of life. We hear of the death of a person, and we say, "O! he is dead! he was so good to *me*," and we mourn, not for him who is dead, not for his awful debt paid, and he *nothing*, but of what he was to *us*, because he was good to us, because in a word he has appealed to our self-love, and not in vain.

"You wouldn't care to go to Penroses?" said Easter rather absently, "for I think the Ancient Mariner is actually meditating departure. She's got an old fossil of a brother who keeps on bullying her to keep house for him."

Hugon's face changed.

To be at Penroses . . . to be near Jem. . . . Heaven opened before her eyes, and she closed them that Easter might not see their expression.

"I'll talk to father about it," said Easter, and smiled. It seemed so funny for any one to be so fond of—Jem. And she had always pitied anyone the shape of whose nose, or the colour of whose complexion forbade sentiment—though their owner's soul might be full of it, and the very way Hugon looked at Jem in company was self-betrayal, her blood ran so clearly at summer warmth when he drew nigh, while the very way she pronounced his name was an open declaration of love— though she did not know it. Life to Hugon just then was like the Norway summer, when the sun sends night and day his vivifying and glorious beams over the frozen ice-world, but after that long bright day comes the endless dark arctic night, no gleam of light, no thrill of warmth . . . and that long night was rapidly approaching to Hugon now, whose only sun was Love.

"Hugon," Easter said thoughtfully, "if your eyebrows had curled more fiercely, your hair been more energetic, and your ears twitched, you would be ever so much more interesting—and wicked. You'll never be more than half-and-half to your dying day."

"Just so," said Hugon, "you mean that in respectability I have lost the power to respond to those primitive passions that sway the lawless, and the lawbreakers equally, but you're wrong. At heart, I'm a savage, but I should have made a decent man—as men go."

"I never could understand your quarrel with Fate for making you a woman. *I'm* quite satisfied."

"A woman is cursed with imagination," said Hugon, "a man has none. Conduct with him takes the place of the ideal."

"They told me I should find you here," said Daddy Gardner's voice in the doorway, and Easter hailed his long nose with joy, and reproached him with having shamefully neglected her.

"You're such a swell now," said Daddy reproachfully, when he had deposited himself in a chair, and gratefully sniffed up the surrounding scents. "Jolly old place, ain't it?" he added, looking round, "but somehow I always expect to find the Shaw gone when I come to call! I don't believe in building under cliffs, and on the edges of precipices, or below reservoirs, Nature first warns you, then slaps your face, and mostly ends by wiping you off the face of the earth."

"Thank you, Daddy, and if that's all you've come to say, you'd better have stopped at home. And another time you come to see me, just have your coat brushed, and get your hair cut."

Daddy looked squashed.

"Now you know, Mrs. Burghersh," he said, "there's a fearful amount of wear and tear entailed on always coming up to the scratch

33*

—let everything slide, and you'll add years
to your life, while wrinkles on your azure
brow will be unknown!"

Hugon slipped away. She had seen Jem
coming. Daddy looked after her, and unconsciously made a face the reverse of
flattering.

"Daddy," said Easter, smiling, "you don't
like women, and that's a fact."

"Well, they ain't interesting in the mass,
shopping, bargaining, chattering," said Daddy
calmly. "The multitude of women affects
man with a contempt for the one, while the
one alone disposes him to think favourably
of the masses. But I know I'm talking
awful rot," said Daddy cheerfully. "So
Strokoff has been down here lately," he added,
colouring uneasily.

"Where—at Fitzwalters?"

The question leaped out like a sword from
a scabbard when its owner's life is threatened.

"I don't know the Fitzwalters lot—or

want to either. I heard he was at Penroses."

"Daddy," cried Easter, furious at his tone, "are you a Pharisee? Now all my sympathies are with those others—the publicans and sinners. 'God be merciful to me, a sinner!' There's a *man* for you! Oh, I could forgive a human vice or two in a man or woman, a passionate crime even, miles before the thousand pitiful meannesses of the so-called religious man or woman! You say of a person, he did such-and-such a thing, wholly bad—Yes, but did he never do anything else —never do anything good or unselfish in his life? You must take the good and the bad deeds right through, strike the balance, and there is the man fit for heaven or hell."

"And Strokoff strikes the balance in favour of hell," said Daddy grimly, who knew what the pursuit of a man who does not love a woman enough to be magnanimous, means.

Easter coloured, but she had begun to think
lately, and now she chose to talk.

"Do you know," she said, after a little
pause. "that the only merciful judges on
earth of women are *good* women and good
men? The good women can't enter into the
temptations that beset the others, and they kiss
the sinner on the mouth because they do not
understand, or perhaps they dimly realise
that woman is the scapegoat of man for all
time——"

"O! come, Mrs. Burghersh," said Daddy,
with a flush on his ugly, kind face, "you
don't look anything of that sort at all, I
assure you — fancy if Burghersh heard
you——"

"Daddy," said Easter, leaning her brilliant,
transparent face on one little hand, and
looking at him earnestly, "have you ever felt,
when you've got everything into a tangle,
that it would be nice to *die*—just to get out
of it?"

" No," said Daddy stoutly, " I can't say I
ever have. Such as life is, one doesn't want
to lose it. One constantly hears people
talking boldly and lightly of taking their lives
if such-and-such things should happen. But
one day a man's heart beats slower, he goes
to a doctor, who looks grave, and a cold chill
passes over the patient that he was far from
feeling when he contemplated taking his last
journey of his own accord. No man likes
interference, even from God, and if his life is
really threatened, he fights doggedly for it to
the end—as you would fight if you had occasion," he added, with a confidence he was far
from feeling, for with a painful heart sinking,
he realized how terribly frail Easter looked—
and how unhappy.

" Let's go and look for Burghersh," he said,
getting up to hide his face, and noting how
on her way to the open windows Easter
paused absently, plucked a flower—smiled at
it, then tried to replace it on its stalk—

came back to herself with an effort, and joined him.

Hugon was saying, "Jem, shall I give you an allegory? A soul sped heavenwards, heavy with a last earthy wish. 'Oh God!' it cried, 'give me this one thing, the care of the one earthly soul I love. Let me go back and comfort her—even if she know me not, let me be there to guard her.' The prayer was granted. Soon he returned weeping. He had found her not sorrowing, but glad, with another man beside her—another man whose image had been deep down in her heart long before he thought he saw his own in it—he had but overlaid it for a time, and was already forgotten."

"Yes," said Jem, puzzled. He knew that he was not clever in the sense that Hugon was, and sometimes her sayings baffled him. This one did especially, he couldn't see any point in it.

Suddenly repenting of her fierceness, she

looked up at the man's strong figure, the fair brown head, and friendly, tanned face, and was glad that he did not understand— had he done so he would not be so worthy of her love.

" Isn't it lovely up here ? " he said cheerily, "the finest house on earth wouldn't give me half the pleasure this prospect does. One may have too many pictures, too many beautiful things around, and one longs to get away from them all, and look clean out from a height like this, with nothing whatever to come between God and you."

His voice was reverent, he had bared his head, and if ever a man of clean heart and life looked fearlessly out upon the future, with the stamp of health and perfect happiness and content on his brow, that man then was Jem Burghersh.

"Here's my sweetheart," he said, as cheerful approaching voices struck on his ear, " the one beautiful thing in the world to me that is not too much, and I can do nothing — nothing on earth but try and deserve her."

But Hugon had disappeared down one of those side alleys that began with so much importance, and mostly ended nowhere, at the Hangingshaw. And in her soul she was calling him, her adored Jem—a fool.

CHAPTER XV.

TOM was willing, but Maria was coy about Hugon's coming to Penroses, for she could not be home for another three weeks at least, and she did not like to think of so ancient a landmark as the Mariner being removed in her absence. The latter had once been described by Dinkie as a person " who put up her lip and baa'd at you," but such as she was she had become an awkward but indispensable piece of furniture at Penroses that everybody, more or less, barked his shins over (especially Tom), no one wanted to lose her.

Whereupon Jem tried strategy, and wrote

to mother-in-law—(I always thought it the only redeeming point in a certain bad man's character, that he forged his mother-in-law's name)—and told her he wanted Easter all to himself for a bit, and the sooner Hugon got ranged, the better he would be pleased—which was a man's way of shewing gratitude for the inestimable gift of a woman's soul—which he did not happen just then to want.

Maria rose nobly to the occasion, and so it happened that one fine morning, Jem, looking after a retreating dog-cart, said "Thank God!" so audibly that the white-faced wretch inside heard him, and Easter called him a brute.

"Well, when you only want *one* woman in the world, where's the good of others fooling round?" he said, quite unabashed, as he snatched her up and carried her into the house, where he petted, amused, and distracted her from her thoughts, till by bedtime she remembered that she had forgotten all day to carry Basil on those nerves that she confidently supposed to be her heart.

One night, as, fragile and almost as unsubstantial as a moonbeam, she lay in Jem's strong arms after dinner, resting quite still, and looking thoughtfully at him at intervals, till like a tired and contented child at last she fell asleep, I think her eyes cleared, and she saw things in their true proportions, saw all the sin of her attitude to Basil and his to her, and from that moment the fever abated, and she became sane.

I suppose that to almost every man it has come at least once in his life to love a woman, to suppose himself loved by her, and to wake up one fine morning and find the woman—gone.

She is there in the flesh, the mocking, laughing thing that has borrowed new charms through her very indifference, but the real essence of her, the something that constituted *love*, and made him a hero to her,

and herself a goddess to him, has fled away
for ever, and will not return.

Sometimes the man's cruelty, frequently
his neglect, or oftener still, some base quality
in himself with which the woman's nobler
nature declines to fuse, has brought about
the catastrophe — but probably he never
really knows himself, he is sure but of one
thing, that the inner heart of her has escaped
him, and only the husk of the treasure
remains in his grasp.

To Jem Burghersh no such awakening
had come, for the simple reason that he
had been content to marry Easter, knowing she did not love him—though on the
other hand he was quite sure that she
did not love anyone else. Had she not in
everything sought his help, even while she
flouted him?   And no matter what *sorties*
she might make, of what extravagances she
might be guilty, she was sure of always
having him to come back to when tired

—and however naughty she might be, to be comforted. And as one unconsciously takes in every detail of a landscape of which one is not at the time thinking, only to vividly remember them afterwards, so a thousand little traits of character, of new and lovable qualities that had passed unnoticed hitherto in Jem, revealed themselves, and every day she came to know him better, to contrast him more favourably with those men she had met in town, who had at first approached her with that insolence which so plainly says, " If I had the time," and who so soon substituted, " If only I had the opportunity ! "

When Easter told Jem one day that he put her in mind of the Bible—the New Testament, be it clearly understood, not the Old, he thought her irreverent, but she really meant it, and insensibly influenced by that strong, steadfast nature, became attuned to better things, and reverted to her neglected needlework, and other sane and simple pleasures that she had forgotten.

And when you know that the slightest thing you do, the very way you pour out a cup of tea, or even say something silly, is inestimably dear and right to a man, it makes you feel comfortable, and well disposed towards that person, and in those days, though Easter did not know it, she was remarkably near to falling in love with her own husband, and might have been entirely happy, but that it is ever the future and the past that hold our jewels—not the present.

Dinkie, who came over as often as possible for a good tuck-out, openly apostrophised them as the " Spoons," and stuck daggers in Hugon's heart afterwards by accounts of their wedded raptures. And the warm spring days (love has no greater friend or foe than the weather) and all the freshness of a world new-made over again, raised Easter's spirits, and drew her out Jem with to explore that kingdom, whose wooded heights and dewy glades were so dear to him, and one day as they sat with their feet in hyacinths and their backs to a silver-barked beech, he spoke to her for the first time of his mother.

She had died young. So much Easter had known by the tablet under a church window upon which was duly inscribed the fact that Margot; had departed this life some twenty years ago, at the mature age of twenty-three.

Jem's father had never looked at that date without a sense of the extreme indiscretion of Providence in meddling with affairs that went so well, for was he not correcting, moulding, and improving his wife into the shape and pattern he had decided on, when death took the improving business out of his hands, and brought her, but half-finished, before her Maker?

Margot had loved dogs and horses, laughter and fresh air, and believed that four walls were built for shelter—not to live in, and giggle in, and practise those ladylike arts for which the world was never one whit the richer, or the happier. There must have been a streak of gipsy blood in her veins, so fond was she of movement, and wandering at the beck and call of her own wayward will, so open to all the sweet influences of nature, so passionately alive to its beauties and surprises; and if she felt too keen a joy in the mere sense of living, did she not suffer with equal sharpness when the conditions under which she lived became unbearable? A handsome face, a cold but charming manner, the reserve of character that causes weakness to pass for strength, and selfishness for force of will, had captivated her heart before she knew what men were; and with the recklessness of a lavishly generous nature, that in giving, never looks to the value of the equivalent received, Margot Burghersh had thrown down her life's treasure royally, only to find out, too late, what a poor

simulacrum of a heart she had received in
exchange.

How should he cut and pare, and stint the
noble nature to his own narrow needs? He
never doubted but that he could do so; and,
indeed, he thought he was getting on very
well indeed, and making a quiet, domesticated
animal of her, when—though she could not
escape from his house, and his company in
the flesh—her spirit fled out through the
narrow gate of death—free. But had it
really escaped? Did not the generous spirit
pass rather into her child, howsoever he
sought to crush and capture it?

From his cradle Jem had been nature's
child, escaping from his cot to wander bare-
foot in the moonbeams, or to dance in the
shadows—knowing every flower and tree in
the place, happy and inconsequent as any
forest creature rejoicing in its own fearless
life, and whose habits he so intimately knew
and imitated, growing up without the

34*

faintest resemblance to the elegant, cold-mannered gentleman who, as years went by, withdrew himself almost wholly into those learned pursuits which often serve as a cloak to hide a man's poverty, and wretchedness of mind and heart.

And at last while his son was abroad, the father's poor apology for a heart had ceased to beat, and Jem after years of travel had come home to his inheritance—and Easter.

" Here she is—poor little soul," he said, drawing from his breast pocket a faded daguerreotype enclosed in an old-fashioned locket, "I'm afraid she didn't have a good time." He paused, "I found a bundle of letters from her to my father——"

Easter slipped her little hand into her husband's, something in his voice told her tears were in his eyes, and somehow Jem, the much-envied master of the Hangingshaw, was only a little boy to her then, who had never known that mother's love and care for which all the treasures on earth will not recompense any poor human soul.

"Jem," she said softly, "I'll try and make it up to you," and they kissed each other like two children, and sat for a long while leaning their heads together, and talking about *her*. The memory of that hour in the quiet glade never left Jem's memory, and in after times came back to Easter so vividly that she could hear over again the thrush's song that "sang their pauses out," remember how the woodland life went on unchecked by their presence, where the green fell palest on the elm boughs, and more vividly on the hawthorns, could see the speckled leaves of the arum thrusting themselves through the earth's mosaic, taste the sharp sourness of the sorrel leaf, and feel the warmth of the south wind as it brought a thousand vernal scents and sounds to her senses, soothing them as only Nature's grand organ notes can.

Jem grudged every minute, every moment

even as it passed. At any hour the summons to his uncle might come, and he must depart, and he had got his joy and he wanted to keep it—and it would be inhuman if at this, the most critical period of their lives, and his first real courtship of his wife, he were to be snatched from her by Fate, which is but a malevolent name for Providence. And Providence played Jem one of its usual unhandsome tricks, and a week after Hugon's departure summoned him by telegram to see a very old man's painful dissolution, when all he wanted was time in which to make a young love thrive.

"I won't go," he cried, throwing down the piece of paper, and looking thoroughly unmanned. "I'm no good—it's the only thing you *can't* help a man to do—to die—and you mustn't come, dear, it would undo every bit of good the quiet lately has done you."

Easter stood quite still with a curious feeling of approaching *loss*, of friendlessness,

different altogether to any feeling she had
ever known for Basil, creeping coldly round
her heart, too timid was it, too vague for
love, and yet was it only the grief with which
one sees depart a *bon camarade* whose trusted
and lovable qualities have endeared him to
you all along the road?

She went up to him where he stood
distracted, and bowed her head till lightly it
touched his breast.   His arms went round
her, and she never forgot their strength, and
the utter sense of safety they gave her im-
pressed themselves physically upon her, so
that in time to come, with many another true
woman she would cry out passionately,

"O! that it were possible after long grief and pain,
  To feel the arms of my true love round me once again."

"The sooner you go, the sooner you will
come back," said Easter, pulling herself
together; "if the poor old man dies, and—and
there will be the funeral, you need only be
gone a week."

Jem looked at her wistfully as he smoothed the hair back from her forehead with one hand, and framed her face with the other.

" Shall I come with you, dear ? " she said.

He thought of the interminable journey, the barrack-like remote castle, without a mistress, of the old Scotch servants who had no idea of comfort, or waiting on a woman, and he dared not take her into such gloomy surroundings, and lest she should urge the point, forbade it.

"You must go to Penroses," he said, " it would drive you melancholy-mad here. I might drop you there on my way," he added, with all a man's ignorance of female packing-up, but this was impossible, and so it happened that within an hour Jem had set out alone, and she never forgot how he came back more than once to take her face in his kind hands, and search it for the love that surely, surely was beginning to give him answer there, and

when at last, too heavy-hearted for speech
he tore himself away, Easter sat down on the
oak settle inside the hall, and oblivious of the
men-servants—wept.

Presently she went into Jem's study, so full
of masculine litter, and picking up his glove
pressed it to her wet cheek, then paused
before a portrait of him in the drawing-
room to think how resolute a man he looked
in it, when with her he was so pliable—so
easy to manage . . . it is usually the
woman he does not love, and not the one he
does, to whom a man shews in the full
strength and beauty of his mind and
character.

CHAPTER XVI

" But ever since I heedlessly did lave
    In thy deceitful stream, a panting glow
    Grew strong within me ; wherefore serve me so
    And call it love ?   Alas, 'twas cruelty."

THERE were rejoicings at Penroses when Easter walked in, just in time for early dinner, and Tom seeing her in her old place, gave that little click of the teeth which always denoted in him unusual satisfaction. Splendid teeth they were, almost redeeming a rather hard mouth—your really successful man in the matter of pounds, shillings and pence, seldom has a beautiful mouth and chin. And a true father, though he may grumble at his overflowing brood, does not wish to see one seat empty, one curly head absent, and never quite forgives the son-in-law who has stolen one bright face from his board. Tom had now almost forgiven Easter for taking French leave of him last year, and when he bent his head to say grace, looking down at the hands (albeit those of a gentleman) that were a mute protest to the do-nothingness of his family, some of the old look on his face when " he owed not any man " came back, and sunshine was the order of the day.

Maria's place and several high chairs were empty, it is true, but it is a melancholy fact that a house conjointly ruled by two persons not always of one mind, goes much more comfortably with one or other of its heads absent, and Easter found a cheeriness in the atmosphere altogether foreign to it when absent keys, and Tom's fulminations thereon, formed the sauce to every family joint.

The outgoing Ancient Mariner beamed on her favourite pupil though the tears that with her betokened pleasure, sitting as far as possible from the in-coming Mrs. Satan who

had arrived, as Dinkie declared, with a bag-
full of brand new tricks, and more amazingly
sinful than ever. The only one silent in all
that cheerful company, Hugon had felt the
coldness of the air when she approached
Easter, and had not trusted her voice to
enquire for Jem—Jem, for a sight of whom
she had sickened a whole week.

Somehow Hugon fell out of the procession
presently formed round the grounds, including
Bunkulorum, who forebore to pepper any
of them with Shakesperean pop-guns, and
to Nan's huge satisfaction, Jem's name remained well to the fore, and whether as kind,
or absurd, or decidedly *thinner*, occupied the
very first place in Easter's conversation from
lawn to stables, and round again by the
piggeries, home.

She was still full of her subject when (Nan,
having gone off to the school-room, Bunkulorum and the Snapper to the grammar school
and Dinkie to his much-loathed 'oss 'air), she

gravitated to the Green-room, which was usually the safest from intrusion in the house.

The green jalousies were closed against the sunshine, the air was sweet with the breath of growing flowers, in the soft gloom she saw no one as she came quietly in, and shut the door behind her.

A girl in a pink cotton gown . . . who had played a game of " Touch-last " with him in a black one . . . who had wept before his eyes in a dusty tallet . . . was this the woman of the world, who had shewn herself as clever at guarding her heart as he had been at hardening his, and by the *flambeau*-light of whose matchless colouring the town-bred beauties had shewn like mere prentice freaks of Nature, all save Lala, whose colourlessness made her charm?

There are women freshly come to a new estate who write married all over themselves, in their faces, on their clothes, who even intone in their voices the announcement that they are the lawful property of some man, invisible perhaps, but through them constantly asserting his existence. There are other women who belong to themselves alone, and are in a sense, impersonal, so that you cannot tell from their appearance or conversation if they are married or single, and Easter was one of these latter.

These first impressions passed through Basil's brain in a flash, the next gave him a new Easter, who was interesting, as are the rarer sort of women, more for the things that she had not done, than for those that she had, and whose loveliness as she now stood before him, reached that highest point of simplicity, distinction.

He had the immeasurable advantage of seeing her first—the girl who had fevered him as he had fevered her, whom he had longed to see, and sternly fled from, whom he would not trust himself with since their broken friendship in Town, and of whose presence to-day at Penroses he was ignorant, or he had never entered its doors.

He rose, and she started as he came forward, but where were the anticipated tremors, raptures and fears of this passionately longed-for moment, now so unexpectedly sprung upon her ?

A natural greeting rose to her lips, and as he took her hand, she caught herself thinking that the Mediterranean depths of his eyes were not so blue as usual, or half as true as some grey ones she knew of, and surely that waist-coat was not in his usual perfect taste . . .

" We have missed each other very often," she said, when they were seated opposite each other, and he saw that she was looking at him eagerly, alertly, no, not at him, but at the chair in which he was sitting, the same one Jem had occupied when he made himself into a ridiculous pin-cushion to please her.

She smiled at the recollection—at something, as Basil saw, quite outside himself, and his personality, and a certain anger came into his face as he looked at her.

"I have been very unfortunate," he said coldly, and Easter thought how cross he was, and how much less really good - looking than Jem. Her spirits rose at finding how little power he had over her, at discovering how much wrong one can do in imagination, yet keep perfectly cool and untempted when face to face with the reality. Then she remembered how good he had been to her father, and said :

"Do you mind telling me if it is you who have saved the Chief and all of us " (she forgot to say " them ") " from ruin ? "

" No," said Basil, with a haughtiness Easter had never seen in him before, " I merely introduced him to someone who could be of material assistance to him. He is not nearly so involved as he at first supposed," and proceeded to give her some details that she did not in the least understand, for if she wanted business, she should have it, he thought savagely, a cold-blooded little devil—throwing him into a fever as she had done, and treating him anyhow when at last they met.

" And so, you see, what I have done is a mere nothing, after all," he concluded, telling the lie valiantly, just as Nan peeped in, saw and heard the distant terms upon which the pair were, and thinking everything safe, beat a hasty retreat.

He called after the child, with a sudden change of look and voice that gave him back all his old charm, but she did not hear him. Who has not seen that lightening of the whole face when a folded brow is relaxed, and the soul is there? And though Basil had not quite forgiven Nan her untimely appearance in Town, love her he must and did always, and the tie that knit them together was not to be broken.

Never a man with a more fastidious taste

than this one, with the English face, the Russian heart, for he wanted the loveliness of one, the character of another, the soul of a third, and the fire and *vim* of a fourth all united in one and the same woman, though if ever he did combine them, he would discover that all these charms were merely negative wants. He had turned too many pages in the book of woman, finding a strong family likeness on every page, to expect anything new, and there is little curiosity among seasoned men in matters of love; to them it is all so stale, and they never cease to wonder at, and pity the freshness of feeling that a woman brings to the dull old theme, whereas ambition, sport, peril, the game of chance, will always stir a man's blood, and fall each moment into new and kaleidoscopic forms of charm.

Basil had sprung up in search of Nan, but when he came back with :

"Is Burghersh here?" in his mouth, he

found himself alone, for, with a dexterity born of long practice, Easter had pushed back the jalousies, and taking the window sill, as it were in her stride, had vanished.

CHAPTER XVII.

" Perverse mankind, whose wills created free
Charge all their woes on absolute decree."
—Homer.

Basil's business with Tom Denison tarried.
He was in his old quarters at "The George,"
and but that Nature's clock stood at spring,
not summer, they might all have rubbed their
eyes and vowed they had but napped—only
to find Penroses had been touched with a
magician's wand during that forty winks,
for Penroses in the month of May — a
forward, not an east winderly May—was a
something too entrancingly lovely for description, making even the Shaw, with its dells and
glades, its terraces and moor, fade into a
mere monotony of greens, and this though
the Hangingshaw covered miles, while Tom
Denison's garden was no more than the heart

of a country town, scooped out for his sovereign will and pleasure.

Only whoever planted the borders of his covetous lawn had been a spendthrift, and kept one month only in his mind, planting the May-trees thickly, not forgetting laburnum, and lilac and syringa, and had drawn, across the wall that ran at right angles with the library, a net-work of wistaria, that lovely wanton among garden flowers who bursts upon the world in such haste that she has ne'er a leaf with which to hide her perfumed loveliness! And once Nature had given the signal, the colours raced each other, never stopping by night or day, so that when the pink May tree was well alight, one but a little farther away caught up the fire in vivid rose colour, and so kindling and dwindling, turning aside to scatter, in palest gold, long ringlets of laburnum, to flush with reddish mauve the lilac plumes, and hold its breath as it passed the white, barely touching the heart of the syringa, but turning to glory the tan of the young beechen leaves, quivered at last like a beacon fire in the crimson double-May that lies hard by the old elm, on the left-hand side of the gravel path. The garden flowers hid themselves, they were of no account in this prodigal feast of colour—only {the lilies of the valley held their own, and Easter was kneeling by, and parting their green 'leaves, and thinking how much wiser they were than the wistaria whose translucent clusters had already begun in places to wither, when she looked up to see Basil beside her, every whit as fresh as the morning and herself.

"Isn't it delicious?" she said, with a little sigh. "Because, you know—it's *stolen*."

He followed her thought, which was a little vague even to herself. She meant that every scrap of happiness we wrest from time and tide is filched, and therefore precious.

"If only it would last," he said, from mere

force of habit settling his cummerbund instead of a waistcoat, "but Life is made up of interruptions — one stops in the middle of a tragedy to listen to the muffin-man going down the street. And to think that I was never in a real garden before," taking off his hat, and looking round him with the most intense satisfaction, as he drew in a deep breath of lilac-scented air, " and that there are poor devils riding in the Row this morning, who fancy they are enjoying themselves!"

"As you have done, and will do again," said Easter, arranging her nosegay, or button-hole, or whatever it might be. There was this comfort at any rate, that they talked to each other like human beings now, and this habit of being natural had grown upon them of late, for often what is impossible to us in December and March, we say and feel with ease in balmy May.

" *I* think the box-seat on a coach would be worth all these—things," and her eyes

swept the wide, vivid circle of loveliness—
she had seen it so often!—disdainfully.
"These lilies are too sweet, and when they
decay—I've seen women who make me think
of decayed lilies in your London—have not
you?" she added, as she gave him some of
the fresh ones, and stuck the others in the
waistbelt of her white gown.

On Mrs. Burghersh's left hand was a
garden-glove, in her whole air there was a
youth, an irresponsibility that forbade the idea
of her being married, and this struck Basil at
the moment so forcibly, that he enquired
how the Hangingshaw managed to get on
without her?

"There is a housekeeper," said Easter,
throwing back her head, and laughing with
the irrepressible delight of a child who is
thoroughly enjoying itself. "She *thinks* she's
the real mistress of the Shaw, and that I'm a
mere interloper, and I *know* it. She rustles as
she walks—there's a rich store-cupboard smell

about her—port-wine, you know, and mince pies, and mulligatawny soup, and things of that sort, and when she speaks, you hear the jingle of countless keys, and there is one little dent in her cheek where I'm sure the butler has kissed her daily during these last thirty years ! "

Basil laughed. In some odd way he was a constant stimulant to women, putting them on their mettle, causing them to display unexpected powers and graces, that ennobled them in their own eyes, and of course him in theirs. Now it had never struck Easter before that she might be amusing—the one, the only desirable gift left on earth (save money), and she glowed towards her sun accordingly, then to cool herself drew down a great bough of white lilac, and holding it in both hands, dipped her face in its wet whiteness.

" Shall I give you a wrinkle to pass on to the women you know ? " she said. " Well—

tell them never to use cosmetics of any kind, but walk in the rain as long as their legs will carry them, and let the rain just wash, and wash, their faces to its heart's content!"

Basil shook his head.

"You can make a good skin bad, but not a bad one good," he said, and then their eyes met, and each knew of what the other was thinking—the *mât* whiteness of one particular woman they knew.

"Is it wicked to wish any one dead?" said Easter, chattering away with that pleasure a woman feels when she knows whatever nonsense she talks is *right*, "because, if not, I wish Jem's uncle would *die*——"

"And then Jem would come home. That's why you look so happy. There's a contented look about a woman who has a man to harry —or make happy — when she hasn't, she becomes meagre, restless—she has missed her vocation, and knows it. A man is bound to come home to his tea—if for a whipping or a kiss, there the poor worm is—I don't speak of men who have not moral or home instincts, of course."

" Of yourself, in short."

" Perhaps.   And he'll be delighted to see you looking so much stronger," he added, " than when I saw you in the Green-room— which must be nearly a week ago."

" It seems years," said Easter, " and centuries since——"

She paused.

" Since we played our game of Touch-last," he said.

" Oh! " cried Easter, with something like a shiver, " it was touch-and-go work, but your blood is *alive*—I can understand now why men brave unheard-of dangers, and go to the remotest countries to hunt big game! I would too, if I were a man.   And I shall never pity the ' red-wood dog,' as we call the fox, so long as he is not caught, *bien entendu !* "

She nodded at him impertinently, throwing back her head, and Easter had one of those faces that is lovely in the foreshortening, just as when you hold a candle under one woman's chin, she is charming, while another is hideous; the trick seems to lie in small straight features, and a short upper lip.

Basil laughed, and looked at her in a proprietary way that amused without irritating her. In Jem it would have produced the liveliest desire to kick him.

"Where is Nan this morning?" he said, "she is usually out by this time."

"Hugon is giving her a music-lesson. Have you ever heard Hugon play? It's the one determined thing about her, and makes you feel as Dinkie says, 'that if she *meant* to commit a murder, she would do it!'"

"Then I suppose if she meant Burghersh to fall in love with her, he would do it. Isn't it a wonderful thing?"

"What?"

"That she should fall in love with him like that."

"It is a perfectly natural thing," cried Easter, blazing round on him like a little fury. "It's the only thing she *could* do—if I did it, why shouldn't she?"

"But did you?"

They had stopped in the middle of the gravel path, defiance in the girl's eyes, provoking laughter in the man's, and Easter put both hands behind her back, so intense was her longing to box his ears on the spot.

"How did you know it?" she said, ignoring his last question. "*She* never told you, I know. Neither did Nan."

"It was the way she said—Jem," replied Basil, still with that maddening look of amused enquiry. "There's a peculiar reverence and tenderness in the way she utters it—for instance, you pronounce it in quite a different way."

"And pray how is that?" said Easter so

haughtily, that it suddenly struck this accomplished student of woman, that indomitable pride was after all the ruling characteristic of her character. "If I did not say it as it should be said, then I am the most ungrateful, wicked woman on God's earth to-day!"

How poignantly sweet came the perfume of the red May by which they were standing, it mingled with their thoughts, and passed into their memories as a scent will, while a heart-breaking sorrow is forgotten, and the real duel that had been played hitherto in jest by these two, began from this moment in bitter earnest.

Basil removed his straw hat as in mechanical acknowledgment of a praiseworthy sentiment, and with rather less interest than he displayed when he performed the same office for "God save the Queen."

"O!" cried Easter, rashly, unadvisedly, as they moved on again side by side, "you don't know—you and your Lala—that it is possible for a man to be good without being dull, and that, though it is picturesque and good form to be wicked, the wickedness itself bores you after a time! I never saw people more utterly sick of themselves and everybody else than people I met out in town—just as tired and *jejune* as we all used to get here at Penroses in the winter," she paused and looked round as if she saw only leafless trees and empty flower-beds, through which even the lilac and yellow spears of the crocus had not pierced, "for it is not always Maytime here."

"Your name has always puzzled me," he said. "Were you born in spring?"

"Yes. On Easter day. And for once mother was fanciful, and called me after the day. Don't you miss her taking you walks round the garden? She is longing to come back, but it isn't safe yet, the doctor says. Isn't it a pity the wistaria fades so soon?" She drew a translucent cluster across her lips

"it's something like a life—all the fun first—
that's the flower — then the leaves — that's
repentance."

"To any one as—prudent as you are," said
Basil calmly, "I should say repentance
would never be necessary."

Easter hopped out of the mould, peppered
with flowers, on which she had encroached to
reach the wistaria, as if it burnt her. It is
almost as hateful to be called discreet—other-
wise a hedger—as to be dubbed "nice-look-
ing" — but by a severe effort she restrained
herself and said, "We can't all be——" She
paused, and as we daily do, substituted one
thing or person, for another—"Nans. And
Nan is a whole-souled idiot. That is what
Dinkie called her this morning — and I
should not like to come the cropper that
Nan will come—and over her best instincts
too, if she gets into the hands of the wrong
man."

"A woman nearly always does that."

"And a man?" cried Easter scornfully. "*He* runs through the letters of the alphabet —spells it backwards—picks out the A or Z he has finally decided on — and makes it' miserable."

Basil was silent. Now there is the pause of dulness, and the pause of strength, when dulness measures the difficulty, and quails, and when strength slowly gathers itself together, and overcomes it.

They had come now to those Green-room windows that made such admirable full-length mirrors in which to view oneself, and Basil, looking at their two reflections, thought what a little girl Easter looked—and a ruffled little girl too—as if she had just quarrelled with her favourite doll, as he jestingly told her. But the Abbey bells chiming the hour suddenly claimed her attention.

"The post is in!" she said, looking up at him with the glad triumph of a schoolboy who knows his "tuck" is round the corner, and she disappeared like a flash of greased lightning into the house.

"Jem," he said with a look of intense disgust, as he got out his cigarette case, " to be beaten by a—*Jem !* "

CHAPTER XVIII.

" I stooped, methought, the dove to take,
    When lo ! I saw a bright green snake
    Coiled round its wings and neck.
    Close by the dove's its head it crouched,
    Green as the herbs on which it couched,
    Swelling its neck as she swelled hers."

LALA's letters arrived at intervals, addressed with a bold precision that argued her intimate knowledge of Basil's character, to the " Royal George." He did not reply to them, and she did not even know he was there, but was sure of it all the same, and if she ironically congratulated him on his present happiness, allowed him to see that she did not expect it to last.

The newspapers had informed her of Jem's attendance on an exalted relative, and save that the *venue* was Penroses, and not, as she

36*

supposed, the Hangingshaw, she knew as precisely what was going forward as if she were there herself. And Basil would come back to her to be—amused. Meanwhile she tried to interest herself in a man who was attracted by her reputation, not herself, and failed.

Jem, watching by the bedside of the man whose eyes mutely implored those around to forgive him for being so inconsiderately long a-dying, thought incessantly of Easter, but always of her as sitting beside him in the glade; the daughter of Margot, who would have loved her, as she would have loved Margot. His mind hardly ever glanced at her as in Basil's company—as she often must be, since her father's business required the Russian's presence at Penroses. And Jem was sure now that he understood Easter better than any one in the world did—so sure that if an angel came down from Heaven and warned him, he would never dare to doubt

her.   He had got to the core of her heart,
which was pure as heaven.

But meanwhile he chafed and longed to
return to her, far away from the spring in
that upper chamber of the gloomy castle, but
from which he took long, long excursions in
the spirit through his woods with her, or
climbed with eager steps those terraces that
seemed ever to make freer his existence, a
part of creation even as the dim coast-line
that seemed to merge itself into the infinity of
heaven itself, and his absence was lamented
by more than one person, notably by Daddy
Gardner who coming over high cockalorum to
Penroses, found himself decidedly out in the
cold, and those erstwhile enemies, Basil and
Mrs. Burghersh, as he expressed it, " thick as
thieves."

It worried the long-nosed, strenuous-faced
Daddy, and he revolved many schemes in his
mind for awakening the young pair to a sense
of what was decorous, but could hit upon

none, till finding himself alone with Easter
at an odd moment, he blurted out his
warning, then fled from the storm he brought
down on his devoted head — and did not
come again.

Nan was never to be seen. Hugon seemed
to have kidnapped the child under pretence
of teaching her. Tom Denison was always
away, Maria and the Shavers still at the sea,
Melons at boarding-school, Dinkie absorbed
in 'oss 'air, Bunkulorum and the Snapper at
the grammar-school, and through the long
hours all the loveliness of that May garden was
for two persons alone, Lala's best young man,
and Jem's wife.

Nan choked down her dim misgivings with
the certainty that Easter watched every post
in with the ardour of a lover. She really saw
less than anyone else (save Tom) of what was
going on, and only lamented Hugon's energy
in teaching her things she did not want to
know, and which would adorn her inelegant

self about as much as a little powder disposed
upon the face of a blackamoor.

She was moreover somewhat preoccupied
by an amazing fact that had made her walk
on air, she had received a compliment.
Sitting on the top of a haystack one morning,
weeping on account of her ugliness, which had
just been forcibly presented to her, she over-
heard one stable-help say to another (who had
apparently acted as eavesdropper) that for his
part, he couldn't see Miss Nan was so ugly
after all—she'd got the beautifullest dancing-
legs he ever saw in his life!

Tom wondered irritably why Strokoff did
not go. It might have been observed that
Tom was not quite at ease with Basil, who
had lied to Easter as to the extent of her
father's obligations to him, and no matter how
delicately such favours were conferred, Tom
weakened at sight of this earthly Providence,
and as men the two no longer stood level.
And Hugon's masterly manipulation of

matters prevented his being aware of the
amount of time Easter and Basil spent
together, and the maids and Sweet William
smiled indulgently. If there is anything on
earth servants heartily co-operate with, it is a
little unlawful love-making, if they are not
"bluffed" by the chief actors, be it understood, but take them into your confidence,
and they will die rather than betray you.

Here it was above board, quite innocent,
but extremely dangerous, and if ever an old
man by shuffling off his mortal coil could
do another a signally good turn, that man
was Jem Burghersh's uncle. Yet a fortnight
passed, before the worst minute that can come
in any man's life was over.

Maria had some bad moments when she remembered that Hugon's waist was not like the
Mariner's, horrific to the male eye, and she did
not share Dinkie's admiration for the character
of Tom Jones. Privately she thought all Toms
were pretty much alike, and did not trust

one of them. However, it wanted now but three days to her return — and then the " procession," as Dinkie politely called it, of children, babies, nurses, dogs, Noah's Arks, with live samples of its contents, and the rest of it would arrive. And Jem's uncle having paid his last debt, Jem might be expected home at latest within a week.

Some of Easter's joyousness left her as the day grew near, and the table-land on which she frolicked seemed to recede under her feet, bringing her to the edge of a sharp precipice, at which everything stopped—nor did she dare to look beyond.

It had come now to the very last night, and in the drawing-room, a long and many-windowed apartment, the loveliest of all the rooms at Penroses, Hugon was playing " Musica Proibita " without any accompaniment of song, but with a genius, a searching pathos that made the soul of the girl who sings over and over the prohibited love words of her banished lover rise in a wail of inextinguishable regret, of insatiable longing and baulked passion that haunted at least one of the hearers' hearts and memories for all time.

Nan had stolen up close, and was drinking eagerly in the whole passionate love-story. Some music melted the very heart within her, and her thoughts embraced all who were in sorrow, and she longed for them to be happy too. At such times she forgave everyone who had wronged her, only wishing that they might love her instead, and her whole soul went out in a wave of love and pity to all human kind, while the mingled joy and agony of living overflowed her soul like a generously-filled cup—and she wept.

Who that has seen a vast multitude spell-bound, enraptured, a prey to the sweetest emotions, would rather not be the man who wrote the intermezzo of " Cavelleria Rusticana " than one of the crowned kings of the

world? The orator upon whose words a vast
populace hangs, the singer whose voice un-
locks the gates of heaven, the musician who
can by his notes speak straight from his soul to
the souls of millions, who shall match them in
power, or what great writer or painter, or
sculptor can ever establish the electric sympathy between themselves and those who
enjoy their master-pieces, as do these others?

Tom did not care for music, and shared
the feelings of those dogs who always uplift
their voices in howls when approached by
sweet sounds, and he had long ago beat a
retreat to the dining-room, and the comforts
of tobacco and whisky, so that save for
Easter and Basil, who sat a little way apart
together, others in the long dimly-lit room
except the player and Nan there were none.

Basil knew the words well, Easter found
them in her heart, and Nan, not knowing,
understood them also.

" Vorrei bacaire i tuoi capelli heri,
Le labbra tue e gliocchi tuoi severi,
Vorrei morir con te angel di Dio,
O bella innamorata, tesor mio.

*   *   *   *   *   *

Stringuimi, o cara, stringuimi al tuo cor
Fammi provar l'ebbrezze dell 'amor."

"Amor." It sounds the same in every
language under heaven, the blind, the deaf,
the dumb know it, and it lingered in the
minds of those who listened, when Hugon
plunged suddenly into wild Hungarian strains,
recalling that enthralling music which the
Tzigans draw from their violins and cymbals,
such melody as stirs the heart to its utmost
depths, and penetrates to the very marrow of
one's bones, and while sending exquisite
thrills through the whole body, somehow
lifts the soul to the highest heights of
Heaven.

When at last those throbbing notes, indefinitely prolonged, ceased, Basil turned his
keen dark face and looked at Easter, lying

in the midst of a heap of chocolate silken cushions, with a falling fire of pink topazes on her breast, looked at her till their eyes met, and fierce, lawless, compelling, there gazed out at her that which the good woman trembles at, and seeks to keep back, that the base one rouses, and fosters by every unholy artifice in her power. For a moment only she saw it, then Basil leaped to his feet, and fled as one pursued by the Furies out into the cool night.

As a rule he did not feel the power of music, but when a man is, if only temporarily, under the influence of a woman, what affects her, affects him also, and Hugon's demon-playing had roused a kindred devil in him, and so—and so—the black drop in him had been stirred, ay, but it should not spread to a sea!

The breeze fanned his brow, and clearing the mists from his brain, also dissipated his passion. He laughed at himself for a madman, as he went with swift step down the wet lawn, and brushed against the chairs in which he and Easter had been sitting that afternoon. . . . Easter—Easter, it had been nothing else but Easter these past fourteen days; she had begun to form part of a habit, and therefore hard to do without . . . it is in the little things, mere homely trifles, that a woman does for a man, that he gets to love her intimately . . . that he gets used to her, and so takes the first step towards wanting her always . . . or at least until he does not want her at all.

But he did not want Easter, he was quite sure of that; wounded pique, desire, obstinacy, a determination not to be beaten—a mixture, in short, of all the worst traits in his character, artfully fomented and kept alive by Hugon, had detained him beside this girl, and made him exert his utmost influence to make her love him, but as to letting himself go, to allowing himself to be mastered, he laughed aloud at the thought, as he stood under the trees where she, a flitting lure of most delicious promise, had beckoned him, and now the same fever with a difference was upon him—and he longed to hold her, if but for one moment, in his arms . . . the sweet that is out of our reach how sweet it is . . . yet when, perchance, after some such long search and suffering as Endymion's, it is ours, does it not vanish quickly into that limbo of forgotten things which we are pleased to dignify with the name of disillusions ?

There is a story told of a lover who, on returning, complained bitterly of the trembling of a plank by which he had crossed over to his beloved.

" But you did not complain when you came over," reproachfully said the waiting-woman who held it.

" You fool," he said, " that was before—this is after."

And that momentary desire, first beneath the trees that night when Easter had eluded him, and again in the moonlight's glamour, had been as it were crystallized, made permanent by infruition, whereas had it been gratified, he would probably have been bitterly disappointed, and in any case have long ago forgotten her. For a man is so, that he always remembers the woman he cannot get, and straightway forgets those that he can.

It is the unknown that fills our thoughts, the mysterious that commands our highest faculties of search, and we turn away from the page clear with beautiful meaning to the hieroglyphics of a tortuous riddle that we shall be none the wiser or better for painfully seeking to learn the meaning of, and for which we have no use when we have learned it.

And if it were not for the doubt, the enchantment, thrown over that instinct which man calls love, how would he find courage to love, to marry, to endure the thousand stripes

and punishments that may be inflicted on the
heart that he puts naked into another's
keeping? It is one of the most felicitous
frauds ever invented by the Final Cause, for
the cozenment of poor humans, that by this
same glamour men and women should be
hoodwinked into becoming careworn citizens
and citizenesses; they would never do it,
these poor human souls, with open eyes,
therefore are they blinded, that the world
may still go round,

"And the individual suffers, and the race is more and
more."

Basil cursed Hugon and her Tzigan
melodies . . . prohibited music indeed,
catch that icicle Easter singing over to
herself anything *he* had ever said to her
. . . there was the rub, that she had kept
her head all through; had she seemed ever
so little embarrassed at so unexpectedly
seeing him, he might have kept cool himself,
but she had defied him into doing his best—

or worst—to make her love him, and even
now he did not know with what result . . .
not even after that burning look they had
but now exchanged.

Of wooing in its ordinary sense between
them, there had been none. He had offered
her no violence or tenderness of love, but
had apparently only taken up that interrupted thread of friendship in which they
had come to know and admire each other
better, which Nan's appearance in town had
summarily broken.

And but for Hugon's superb diplomacy in
now throwing them together, they might
have continued proud and alienated—as after
the Park Lane incident they had remained—
to the end. He wished to God that they had,
for what possible end could come to him in
this thing but humiliation and defeat? This
was no summer's day intrigue, that dies
naturally in its own fulfilment, and to give
himself away, to let himself go for nothing,

was altogether out of the calculations of this finished man of the world, to whom ambition was so much more than love, and who had so carefully kept heart out of all his enjoyments until now.

It was Jem whom Easter really loved, whom she had preferred all through, though she did not know it, and as to her fancy for himself, Basil doubted if it had gone very deep. He knew—none better—that there must be two men to make a woman's state really emotional, one whom she suffers to make love to her, and one whom she denies, so that between the two, love never leaves her. No wise man desires to be loved seriously—he flees from such devastating flame as from a plague—it is the overflow of the serious passion he wants to make him comfortable, not the passion itself.

Now, if it had been Nan? . . . Involuntarily he looked upwards, and the thousand eyes of the night answered his, the

37*

exhalations of swelling bud and twig, of
growing green things cooled his soul as the
swift movement to and fro had soothed his
restless body, the one human thing in this
quiet hour, that moved unquietly. A sense
of his own nothingness, of the paltriness of
his life and aims, of the evanescence, more, of
the sin of such a passion as his, was suddenly
borne in upon him, and a contempt for himself,
that included Easter, moved him—for what
place had such poor mockery of love as
theirs, among the grand doings of the
universe ? Nan was in harmony with it, as
he once had been, but now the meanest thing
that crawled was nobler than was he to night
. . . and he grew sane as he stood there
in the darkness, and thrust his desire from
him, crying out to God that he would have
none of it, that he would go hence, and regain
that command of himself which in his life's
wrong-doing he had deliberately refused to
acquire.

It was a weary man, his hair damp with dew, his face cold and pale with past struggle, who presently re-entered Penroses, and on the very threshold found his way barred by Hugon.

"What do you want?" he said roughly, and would have passed her.

"Nan wants you; she is upstairs."

She pointed upwards to the drawing-room, and spoke the lie bravely. He had never disobeyed any wish of Nan's yet. With lagging, unwilling footsteps, he went.

CHAPTER XIX.

" As I sat on the deep sea sand,
I saw a fair ship nigh at land.
I waved my wings, I beat my beak,
The ship sunk, and I heard a shriek,
There they lie—one, two and three."

EASTER sat motionless as a statue long after Basil had gone out, and Nan retired to bed. If she needed illumination, if she wanted to know what she was, and might yet become, Basil's eyes had told her, and stripped naked of all pretence, all deceitful show of friendship, Basil's passion declared itself for what it was, one that no true woman could be proud of awakening.

She was Jem's wife . . . his wife . . and another man misled by her caprice, had dared to look at her thus. And whose was the fault? She had scoffed at principle, trampled on duty, laid herself out for admiration, and Basil had taken her at her own valuation—and told her so. It was not love—not love, this scorching flame that bit and stung her soul . . . ah! but there was no monotony in this, as in Jem's love; here were excitement, peril, passion, all that makes life course through the veins at its fiercest and keenest, and urging her onward to Heaven or hell—all one, so Basil and she were together. But to-night there suddenly recurred to her Daddy's flushed face, when he had dared to warn her, and only got severely snubbed for his pains.

He had felt it keenly, for his love for her was a very real factor in his life, but his only reproach to her as he turned away, had moved Easter.

"If ever you want a friend, Mrs. Burghersh," he had said, "come to me. I'll help you; right or wrong to other people, you will never be wrong to me," for as he saw her then, the blood ebbing and flowing in her cheeks—that vivid blood which surely owed not to earth its heavenly dye — she looked so transparently fragile that a great fear almost stopped the boy's honest, blundering heart, and he cursed Jem for a fool.

We are all too apt to rate a man by his effect on others, and Easter had undoubtedly been influenced by Basil's position and extraordinary distinction in Town, while the extent of his personal charm was only to be gauged by the way other people, in contradiction with him, irritated her, and put her on the worst possible terms with herself.

And she was deeply grateful for what he had done to save her father, and as they dawdled about the garden, or conversed, in the real sense of the word, for the first time in their lives within doors, he got that chance —for which he had latterly become keen— of making her feel the power she defied. And Hugon—probably no average person is

conscious of taking his first downward step—
to himself only he appears to be tempted to
do so; yet the step is taken.   Usually he
would not take it at all, but that circumstance
decides it for him—circumstance, that thief
of good intentions and juggler with our most
honorably laid-out plans, which has brought
about more sin than all the deliberately-
intended evil-doing in the world.

But Hugon knew what she was doing
very well indeed, and Jem's good influence,
that had been to her dark soul as one of
those reflected lights that you may sometimes see far beneath you in a pool among
black sea-weeded rocks, went out shuddering,
as Basil having fled and Nan departed for the
night, she laid her hand on Easter's shoulder
and stooped down to look intently into her
face.

" What is it ? " she said.

Some women might have been moved from
their purpose by the look Easter turned on

Hugon, but as this woman had deliberately pushed her down the steep incline of temptation, so she now felt no impulse to stay the strong hand uplifted to dash the girl to perdition.

"See here," she said austerely, and drew from her breast a small packet that she placed in the girl's hands, "you have often asked me for Basil Strokoff's letters written to you at Fairmile, and I told you they were destroyed. I told you a lie. Read them in your own room—put on your wrapper, and come back to me here."

Easter trembled violently, and held the letters fast.

"He must not find me here," she said.

"He is smoking with your father; he will not come upstairs again to-night."

But Easter was already half way to the Blue room, in the midst of which she stood trembling, and bathed in the queer light that came through the bluish-green glass that shaded the lamp.

Women are sometimes as much alike in moments of strong excitement as black and white men are in growing alike a white beard when they are old; you expect the black man's beard to remain black always, but it doesn't, and a true woman always wants to take off her trinkets before giving herself up to the luxury of reading a love-letter, so Easter tore off her evening gown and jewels, threw on that immoral white silk wrapper, of which mention has already been made, and stood up to read the love-letters, only four in number, written to her just upon a year ago.

Characteristic, reckless, impassioned, chivalrous even in their boldness, they were the letters of the hawk to the dove, the man of the world to the *ingénue*, yet they were flesh and blood too, and struck a chord of romance in Easter, that had never been wakened before, and she thought how strangely they contrasted with that coldness in Basil which had distinguished his early conduct to her at Penroses, though, if they meant anything, they meant that he had loved her right through, at Fairmile, at Penroses, in Town, and again with ever cumulative strength at the present time.

He had not loved Lala, he had loved *her*. And even the proudest woman's heart may bow to a momentary longing almost as passionate, as intense, as the man's masterful desire of possession, and though she feel it to be shameful when her limbs grow weak, and self-mastery is ever so slightly threatened, is she not in such moments almost half compensated for the disadvantage of her sex?

She tried to think of Jem, but he was blurred, a mere shadow. Basil, as he had looked at her to-night, as he had but now spoken to her—(were not these written words fresh and living as if just uttered?)—filled all

her horizon, and so possessed her that she did
not even know how she got to the drawing-
room, or even that she was there at all, till in
a long mirror she saw herself, white as snow,
with deep, dark eyes full of fire, and soft lips
that trembled as if intoxicated by their own
speech as they whispered :

"He loves me . . . I'm afraid. . ."

The enormous sleeves of her wide white
wrapper, caught up to the very shoulders,
showed her bare arms clasped above her head,
and crushed down the dark rings of hair with
that whiteness ; beneath the masses of Mechlin
lace her breast heaved, and the curve of her
young neck shewed, white as the drifted
snow.

A door closed behind her ; she turned and
half stretched out the letters, as in witness.
"He *loves* me," she said again, and all disordered with emotion, moved a step forward,
to find herself face to face, not with Hugon,
but Basil !

Cold—with renunciation in his eyes—he looked at her—at the letters, knowing them for his own—knowing also that, kindled by them for the moment at least, and at last, Easter loved him.

At sight of him her breath came short—her limbs trembled—shame and fear were in her eyes, and all the young allures, the moonlight beauties of sorrow were revealed in her . . . sorrow of his making, and a man loves the sight of his own handiwork, even if if it be evil, and all at once the loveliness that he had but coldly admired, took passionate hold of him ; for out yonder, under the stars, he had reckoned without the woman, ay, and without the man in himself, and his face changed, and broke up in convulsions. The crucial temptation of his life had come, and he went down before it, as all along, knowing the flaw in his character, he had been morally certain he should do, if he suffered himself to be tempted. What he wanted, that he must

have—would have—never counting the cost,
and now he had got beyond himself, and made
no pretence at self-control. He wanted
Easter, and told her so in a way to thrill her
with mingled ecstasy and terror—his eyes and
voice carrying to her no meaning but love—
love boundless—all subduing—all entreating,
sweeter than oblivion—stronger than death—
fierce as the current that sweeps the mariner
on to the jagged rocks that await him.

For awhile she heard him as one in a
stupor, then, when as with a leaping gesture,
he would have snatched her in his arms, she
stepped back, and lifting one arm with a
wild, imploring gesture :

"O ! *poor Jem !* " she said.

That poignant note of anguish—of appeal
to him against herself, arrested him where he
stood. So might Nan have spoken, or that
better angel whose promptings he had
become too deaf to hear, so had the stars
counselled him, but now they spoke too late,

his passions had mastered him, and he would have gone through a lake of fire after Easter to-night.

"Say you love me, O! my beauty, just once!" he cried exultantly, "say it!"

But she fell back before him.

"Jem," she said pitifully, as one who repeats a charm, or a child in its fear a prayer it has been taught, and ever falling back before that masterful advance, towards the door.

"Jem," he said, "what of him? The poor fool had his chance, and lost it. O! you have led me a fine dance, Easter, but now you are mine. I let you go once—twice —but you shall not escape me again, and I will teach you what love is," and he stooped down and kissed her bare arm so fiercely that all the outrage and shame of an hour ago rushed over her, for though we may bear cruel scourging for love's sake, we must be very sure that it is love himself who scourges us.

"You can teach me nothing," she said, very low, "for I will learn no new lesson save from Jem."

"By God!" he cried furiously, "I will break you, or leave you . . . and I will not leave you!"

He had closed his hand over hers on the door-handle. The fever had ebbed away, and left her cold as ice. Pale as the dead they glared into each other's faces, measuring swords, and seeking each a sign of weakening in the other.

"You frail, beautiful thing," he said in that voice of music which had such power to thrill women's hearts, "how dare you stand up to me like this? It has been a game of Catch-last all through, and now I have caught you—and, by God, I'll keep you!"

Something stirred under their hands, some-one was turning the handle on the other side of the door, and Easter cried "Thank God!" and Basil's face changed to that of a devil.

It was Sweet William, asking if he might put out the lamps for the night, and Basil's hand tightened like a vice on hers as he bade the man begone, and with his lips strangled the terrified cry with which she besought help.

"You thanked God too soon," he said below his breath, as turning he seized her arms and locked them fiercely about his neck.

*　　　*　　　*　　　*　　　*

Below stairs, Hugon, mixing Tom's whisky and water strong, and encouraging him to the recital of those exploits in the hunting-field for which he was justly famous, once or twice, quite in the wrong place, *laughed*— laughed as fiends laugh, not because they are happy, but because they have reduced some happy soul to their own miserable estate.

The drawing-room lamps were still alight, but the room was empty, and all the house quiet, when having seen neither Easter nor

Basil again, Hugon, accompanying Tom's somewhat devious steps upstairs, herself retired to bed.

*   *   *   *   *

In the dead of night Nan woke suddenly, and sat up. Someone had touched her—had kissed her—the door was shut, but something had just passed through it, she could almost *feel* a palpable presence, and immediately her thoughts flew to Easter, and her body took the direction of her thoughts.

All the passages were in darkness, and only a faint glimmer shewed in Easter's chamber, blue like the hangings of the apartment, and casting a weird light on the bed that Nan saw at a glance was empty — more, that it had evidently not been slept in that night.

The child stood still, at fault—where was Easter? Instinct rather than thought made her turn to the window, and lift a corner of the blind, for she was well aware of Easter's

38*

wild gipsy ways that had only broken out in her, or perhaps on that very account, only since her translation to the well-ordered dulness of the Hangingshaw, and the whim might have seized her to go out into the garden, wild and unfettered as any night-bird or creature there.

Nan flew back to her room, and wasted some time in dressing, owing to the fact that as usual, on retiring, she had hurled each article of her attire to right and left of her, and could find no matches with which to discover the missing fellows to boots and stockings. When at last she was after a fashion, clad, she presented a curious spectacle, though like Maryanne in the song " she'd no idea when she went out, she'd go so *far*."

It did not surprise her to find the lawn door ajar, but as she stood listening, and uncertain which direction to take, to her astonishment, a murmur of voices, faint, but easily to be distinguished, reached her from the direction of the stables.

To run along the shrubbery and dash through the ivied door was the work of a moment. It swung to with a bang, and gave warning of her approach, for on entering the courtyard, and turning involuntarily to the strange spectacle of a lantern hung against the stable wall, Basil faced her, stern and menacing, and when she would have got past him to what she half imagined, half saw beyond, he harshly bade her go back, for she was not wanted here — to go back at once . . .

Nan scarcely understood him . . . this was not Basil—this man whose face was mad and *bad*—whose voice was cruel—who seemed in the grip of some savage and brutal passion that savoured more of hate than love, and perhaps more of revenge than either . . .

" What are you doing with Easter ? " she cried, struggling with him as he held her back, " she is over there. In the dog-cart . . . Where are you going? Easter? *Easter !* "

The cry burst from her very soul—instinct told her that as well trust a lamb with a wolf as her sister with Basil in the mood he was now in, and that, passion-possessed, devil-controlled, deafer than any adder was he at that moment to the voice of reason or wildest supplication. His blood was up—*a man*—neither to hold nor to bind, he dashed her aside as the fierce wind drives a straw, leaped to Easter's side in the dog-cart, and drove furiously away.

Book iii.—The Punishment.

CHAPTER I.

" It is too late to be on our guard when we are in the midst of misfortune."

—SENECA.

THE absence of Easter from the Penroses breakfast-table did not excite comment, but when Nan was also not to be found in the ranks of the prayerful, enquiry was instituted with the result that her clothes— some of her clothes—none of them matches— were reported as missing, whereupon Dinkie inwardly reviling her for discovering some pleasant thing she had not invited him to share, resolved to make things warm for her at the first convenient opportunity.

But a stable help could have told tales of a disreputable old shoe picked up in the

courtyard, and the head groom was scratch-
ing his head in wonder as to where Mrs.
Burghersh's dog-cart and Rufus had got to,
while within doors, the maids were whispering
about a bed that had not been slept in, and
Sweet William made himself master of the
situation by averring that Prince Strokoff's
angry voice had bade him begone from the
drawing-room when he went up to turn the
lamps out last night, and that he was almost
sure he heard Miss Easter's voice cry out
after him to come back. He *had* gone back,
but the door was fast held, and there was a
sound of struggling inside, but the order to
go had been so fierce, he daredn't interfere,
and went to bed instead.

While they were staring at each other, and
being country-bred and dutiful, hesitating to
put into words what town servants would
have fought over each other to say, word was
brought that the dog-cart had been found
knocked to pieces in the road just outside

a distant railway station, while Rufus was discovered taking a morning refresher off a convenient truss of hay, that he had discovered in a truck on a siding.

Dinkie neglected business to stride into the parlour with the news, wrathfully connecting the catastrophe with Nan, who, as he put it, must have gone very much off her chump indeed, to collar the dog-cart and go out driving, the Lord and she didn't know where, but then the moon was at the full, and she was always more cracked at such times than others, and a devil of a shine there would be when the Chief came to find it out, which would be pretty quick.

And she had run away from the consequences, of course—just like a girl when she had made a mess of everything—and he 'sposed she wouldn't come home till she was starved out—and wouldn't she get it hot when she did!

Bunkulorum, who belonged to the class of

persons who see and don't talk, while Dinkie
usually talked and did not see, happening to
be at home with the toothache, quietly remarked that he did not believe Nan had
taken out the dog-cart at all, but probably
Easter, or perhaps, he added in a colourless
way, possibly Basil Strokoff might be able to
throw some light on the occurrence, as he
had disappeared also, or at least his letters
had been sent round from "The George," as
he had not slept there last night.

Dinkie turned first red, then white, tore up
to Easter's room, came quietly back, sat down
—and trembled.

Almost on the instant, Jem Burghersh, who
had been travelling all night, came rushing in,
ardently demanding Easter, and in wildest
spirits, for it is a fact that the funeral of a
person in whom you are not greatly inte-
rested, gives a new zest to life, and greatly
intensifies your appreciation of the joys
thereof, and others to come.

"Easter is—is not down yet," said Bunkulorum, rising to the occasion, but Jem looked
away from their young dismayed faces to
Hugon, who at that moment came in, and he
knew as one does know, without a word,
with scarcely a look, that a great calamity
has come upon him, and as she stepped
swiftly up to where he stood, and looked into
his face without speaking, in the full flood of
his happiness he withered at the look, pierced
to the very core of his heart, which was
Easter. And still she did not speak, any
more than a mother might upon whom is laid
the command to deal death unto her child,
. . . . and before the tragedy of these two
creatures standing eye to eye, the one waiting
to strike, the other to endure, the boys shrank
and dwindled away, leaving them alone.

She never knew, nor did he, how at last
words came, or how she told him. When he
did know, when with all the joyous currents
of life frozen in his veins, the deadly faintness

had passed, that was Nature's revolt against the agony laid upon him, he put her back with a gesture that was grand in its simple unbelief.

"You say that Easter has gone away with Prince Strokoff," he said. "I do not believe it. She was my wife—I know her better than any of you do — I understand her thoroughly, and she never loved him—she loved *me*. She had a fancy for this man once, but that is past, and until she tells me so herself, I will not believe it. I know what my dear wife could, and could not do—and she *could* not do this thing—it is not in her."

Hugon had reckoned without the loyalty of this man—loyalty, the rarest, most priceless quality on earth, yet that was as much enwoven in Jem's nature as the flesh and blood that, commingled, gave him life.

"God help you!" she said, and held out the letters, open, that Easter had left behind, scattered in her flight.

He just glanced at, without touching them, then looked away.

"You call yourself her friend," he said sternly, "and she was always good to you. God forgive me if I am wrong, but I think you have a spite against her."

He looked as one who does not see, round the homely parlour, but a scrap of Easter's needlework that he knew, brought sight back to his eyes, and he snatched it up, and kissed it, then hid the gaily-coloured thing away gently in his breast pocket, inestimably dear to him since it was hers.

Hugon realized then how all her love had been in vain, how it was not even love at all to him, who did not desire it, for a man's selfishness—even the best of them—is the very grain and proof of his manhood, and what he does not want, that he will not have, for to him it is less than dross.

In a moment of time, she saw how beautiful her first conception of love might have re-

mained to all time had she willed it so . . . .
for she could not say like Guinevere:

> "It was my duty to have loved the highest,
>   It surely was my profit had I known;
>   It would have been my pleasure had I seen;
>   We needs must love the highest when we see it. . ."

for she had seen and known the best all along,
and had deliberately chosen the evil. If she
had been true to her first ideal, and saved
instead of betraying Easter, Jem would have
loved her indeed, with that love which is a
crown of glory to a woman, and ennobling
both to him and to her.

There was that in his voice, in his glance,
that was terrible to the woman, for without
accusing, he had condemned her, and she
knew it—the single heart had searched the
double one, and to Jem the whitest virtue of
this woman was blacker than Easter's
blackest sin.

"I don't believe it," he cried out suddenly
and angrily. "I will not . . . I dare

not. . . ." and mad, stubborn, contemptible, call him what you will, the stand he took then, he took right through to the end, so ruling himself that he never even looked on that other side where madness lay.

Hugon dragged herself after him like some death-smitten thing, as he turned to leave her. "The thing had very old beginnings," she said, " and what began at Fairmile could only end one way. These letters that you will not read were addressed to, and replied to, by her before you had ever come home to the Shaw. And why did he follow her to Penroses? You have been blind all through—you are vowing yourself to blindness still. But you have *got* to see—you have got to have it out with your own soul—and some day you will know —will know . . ."

Jem turned aside that she might not see the greyness that crept over his face, and settled there. Easter's deceit about Fairmile had long ago hit him hard . . . but as he had said no word then, so he said none now.

"They have been always together ever since you went away," said Hugon, growing pitiless and beyond herself, as she found she had absolutely no power to move him; "they have met here before, often, when you did not know it—but they had a little shame left, so ran away before you came back. Look for them, as you please, and where you please— but what Basil Strokoff has, he holds, and you will never see her again."

"I shall see her," said Jem, turning a face steadfast and strong to save, as an angel's upon her, "for she will come back to me— wherever she is, and I don't believe for one moment that she has done wrong. She will turn to me in her trouble—and I shall be ready for her—with only welcome and love. If it is a day, a year, or for ever, it will be all the same—the Shaw and I will be waiting for her—but do not dare ever to speak to me of

her again—for you have not been her friend
—or mine." .

He would have left her then, but she threw
herself in his way, and fell at his feet.

"O, my God!" she cried, with such wild
love and anguish as might surely have moved
the hardest heart to pity, but touched his no
whit, "and do you leave me thus? Have *I*
not loved you best?"

"Get up," he said harshly, and dragged
her to her feet, while the shame in his eyes
hurt her, she knowing it not to be for himself,
but for her, and without another word or
look he would have left her, but she threw
herself upon him like a wild cat, and held him
fast.

"Listen," she said, stammering, gibbering
out the words in her mad haste. "You have
taught me . . . all I know . . . I
was a lost, degraded wretch till I knew you,
and if you raised me, I . . . did . . .
you no harm. I only wanted to . . . to

love you.   When you came to Fairmile . . .
I loved you more — and more — *she* did
not love *you*, and it hurt me — and then it
grew and grew .   .   .   and I could not live
without a sight of you.   And all the while it
was Basil she loved—not you——"

"No," shouted Jem, trying with as little
roughness as a man may, to unlock her hands
from his arm.   "She did not, and you—" the
scorn in his grey eyes blighted her, "I
begin to see it all now—you thought, O! my
God, that you would take her place—*hers*—"
he laughed aloud in boundless contempt—
"and it was all a put-up thing between you
and that man——"

The deep hate in him swelled out in those
last words, he trembled violently, and for a
moment tottered on the verge of *seeing*, then
snatched his self-control again, and was calm.

"She was only a child," he said, "a dear
little ignorant child, no match for you and
him, but, please God, you have not done all

the harm you wished, and think. And, whatever your devil's work has made her, I love her with every fibre of my heart, every throb and pulse of my body, and will love her till I crumble to dust. Woman——" every emotion of which man is capable swelled through the deep diapason of his voice, " what had we done to you, that you should serve us so ill?"

"I was a stranger and ye took me in," she said, "sick and ye comforted me . . . but besides all the harm I have done, do you think of what I gave *you?*"

"No," he said, turning wearily to go.

"I gave you," she said, "what a man gave his life to win from me—and could not. You asked me often for the story of my life. Do you want to know it?"

"No," he said again. He was not listening. He was thinking of Easter. If Hugon had not been temporarily mad she must have seen that he did not hear her. It might come

39*

back upon him later, but he did not hear her
—*now*.

"I was alone in the world, my parents had
left me nothing—not even a name. I invented
the one by which I am known. But the stars
in their courses fought against me—whatever
I tried to do right, turned out wrong. Don't
you think it was a temptation to me in my
loveless life, when a man—loved me? First
he was kind to me, and I was grateful—he was
kinder still, and I hated his kindness, and,
one day, one day, when he forced upon me
what would have dragged me down, down,
into a slime where so many butterflies' wings
fluttered, but never rose again—I killed him.
He would have killed my soul—I slew his
body—to save myself—because my inner self
was dearer to me than the baser one—because
if I had let him live, he would have made me
like unto himself, and I chose to give myself
up to torture first . . . and I spent five
years at the *travaux forcés* (she held up her

scarred hands), for they brought it in man-slaughter only. Women came to me in prison, thanked me, blessed me for avenging their wrongs . . . and they were so many . . . no brute was ever so human . . . and now the soul I committed murder to save is lost, lost! for love—pure love——"

Jem closed the door behind him. The woman had already passed out of his recollection. He had gone to wait for Easter.

CHAPTER II.

" It is an easy matter to take away our lives, but a difficult one to wipe out the disgrace of it."

—Thucydides.

A BLACK cloud had swooped down, and settled on Penroses, and in its gloom the older inhabitants stumbled, more or less painfully, through the long, early summer days, and none more painfully than Tom, who raged through his appointed tasks, knowing that the ponderous machinery among which he moved, was Basil's, the very workmen's bodies who plied it, Basil's, ay, and the very soul of him, himself, was Basil's, and that he was doing hireling work for the man who had made an insolent pretence of saving him, to be the better able to corrupt and ruin his daughter, for with all these things had Basil bought Easter's soul. Tom nearly went mad in that thraldom which he could not break till he could find and deliver up to him, his stewardship, *then*—as man to man should the reckoning be between them, and out of Penroses would Tom Denison go, his children at his back, to begin the world over afresh at fifty, and in far worse case than when Basil had interposed to save him from ruin.

But Prince Strokoff was apparently in no hurry to keep an appointment with Nemesis, and consequently left no address when he left England in company with a lady and her maid, a very few hours after he vanished from Penroses. And Jem, who was the proper person to trace the pair, had, after hearing Nan's account of how she had been witness to the elopement, retired to the Hangingshaw, where the world left him, calling him fool and worse names, which he heeded not at all.

Perhaps he *was* mad—inasmuch as what was clear as day to others, he could not see.

So God in his mercy sometimes hides a man's misery from him, lest looking at it full front, he die, but reveals it to him edge-ways, side-ways, in part, but never in its entirety, and so keeps ever a film betwixt him, and his own soul.

And of all the county only one woman grieved for Jem, and in spirit sat with him in his sorrow, and that was Lady Biddy; the rest said that it served him right for marrying out of his own class, and they were angry too at not having closely followed the progress ot the affair, and seen it enacted under their very eyes. It is so almost impossible to believe that anything of consequence is happening in the world, or to our acquaint-ance, that we cannot hear! People may *think* so, to be sure, and So-and-So *may* suffer— perhaps he does—but, dear me, not to the same extent as if we were standing by, and assisting! The grasshopper's squeak in our ears is louder far than the roar of the battle, raging a mile away! In short, the world's affairs are of importance, or *not* of importance, solely in their relation to ourselves. We smile leniently when we hear that a neighbour is angry at being called this and that—silly fellow! why does he mind? It is all chaff, and how thin-skinned the fellow is!—but it becomes a vital matter when somebody says something about *us*—then the majesty of the great " I " is involved, and we are touched to the very quick, for what we were indulgent to in others becomes a crime when we ourselves are accused of it.

The next surprising incident was, that Hugon disappeared. Nobody saw her go, but she took her slender wardrobe, and it was always suspected that Bunkulorum, who flattered himself that his intellectual tastes and hers were in common, and who also belonged, by virtue of his snail-surrender, to her class of Ishmael, felt for her, aided and abetted her, as the empty state of his money box—(investigated by Dinkie, who was wont to require assistance in his *menus plaisirs*)— plainly shewed, though being charged with the offence, Bunkulorum showed his wisdom by preserving that discreet silence impossible to be learned of the fool.

" My husband says I never told him a lie in my life," a woman once said to me, " and it's quite true—for I never tell him anything."

Maria, returning to fresh misfortunes, and heavily hit over her daughter's disgrace, upon which, after the manner of some mothers, she was a little hard, shewed more sympathy with Tom in his troubles than she had hitherto evinced, for here was a real calamity, one that she could see and comprehend, and I befear me, that many a salt tear was stitched into that beautiful needlework in which Maria so conspicuously excelled, and which now became more comfort to her than ever.

The Ancient Mariner, like the dear good

woman that she was, would not desert the family in their misfortune, and came out in splendid style, while in the depths of her faithful soul was rooted the belief that Hugon was responsible for the catastrophe. Nan was nearly beside herself at the blindness that had overtaken her when she required clearest sight, and Maria, going back to her first cold instinct of repulsion towards Easter's friend, blamed herself for having admitted a woman who was never heard to speak of home or people, to Penroses. She could not forgive Easter, but it hurt her when Mr. Denison called down curses on the jade's head, who had first deceived her father, then her husband, and brought shame upon them all under circumstances that made that shame doubly difficult to bear, for the price paid for his rehabilitation before men had been the flower of his flock—Easter. And he scorned and hated Burghersh, both for his inability to guard and keep what he had won, and his present pusillanimous conduct, incredible in a man of honour; had it been himself he would have found and killed his wife's destroyer if he were to be found upon earth, but to sit down at the Shaw, and await the prodigal's return with wide open arms, was in Tom's eyes, contemptible, and the very height of bathos.

Meanwhile, his place in church stood empty, but Maria with true womanly courage took the children with her, and worshipped as before—only she put her pink and peach crêpe bonnets away, and with them much of her matronly beauty and content.

The news of Basil's escapade reached Town almost as quickly as he did, for a local gossip wired the news to Billy, who forthwith started off to Lala, delighted—for all his good nature —as most people are, to be the bearer of ill news.

He found that Pioneer-product of the twentieth century at home, and when he told her, she looked up at him with the serene, dauntless look that had cowed so many enemies, and carried her triumphantly over so many tight places, and smiled, and said:

"*Fool!*"

Only when Billy had gone away, her face changed, and her lips quivered convulsively, for the one vulnerable spot in her heart, the one thing she valued even above her position, was—Basil.

And she hated Easter, for Easter had beaten her, and the attraction must have been extraordinarily powerful to make Basil commit this, the most suicidal folly, of which he had ever been guilty.

It would not last—there was not enough of the devil in Mrs. Burghersh for Basil. And then Lala ordered her carriage, and drove down to see Princess Strokoff at Fairmile.

That lady's house looked a glass palace to a cursory observer, so vast was its winter

garden that, kept always at one tempera-
ture, filled with exotics, and made livable
by every circumstance of luxury, partly
fulfilled her Russian husband's idea of
what was bearable in this land of exile.
Absorbed in his country and its wrongs, with
the *morne* character and fatalistic tendencies
of his race, he lived in a world entirely
unshared by his English wife, who was not
aware how thoroughly their son, beneath
the careless garb of an idle man of fashion,
shared in his father's ambitions and desires,
and for all his English exterior, was a Russian
to the very core of his heart.

His mother had no influence over him, and
did not desire any; had his beauty belonged
to a girl, she would have loved and decked it
gloriously, for the light of her eyes, her soul,
was *chiffons*, and she had been heard to say that
she liked being a woman, to be able to wear
nice clothes. Now, my opinion is, that being
a woman might be bearable if it were not for

the clothes; but no doubt this is purely a
matter of taste, and Princess Strokoff was
emphatically a woman who held the former
opinion, and was, so to speak, ~~held~~ up and
ruled by her habiliments, and could never be
an entirely unhappy creature so long as
sables held their colour and warmth, lace its
cobwebby texture, fine linen its silken soft-
ness, and while she was dressed by the right
people in the right way. Upon all such
matters she brought to bear a matchless taste
and genius for form and colour that entirely
absorbed the little brain she possessed, and
with astonishingly good results, so far as the
pleasure she gave herself and others was
concerned. So that after all she had her
uses, and was admirable, inasmuch as anyone
is worthy of our gratitude who contributes
his mite to the grace and beauty in the world.

And, meanwhile, in Basil's reckless, wayward, brilliant life, was clearly to be seen the
result of his home training. For O!

mothers, a child is what you make him; he must grow up with you, step by step; he is anybody's child just as much as yours, if you let his precious youngest years slip away from you, and it is too late when you snatch at him, crying out, "Love me—you are *my* child!" and only a pitiful silence answers you, for the love is not there—you have omitted to sow the seed of it.

Lala found the Princess in that winter garden that was also a spring and summer one, breathing with pleasure the soft flower-scented air that was a necessity of her existence, and at the same time performing the whole duty of woman if that duty lay in delighting the eyes of the beholder.

She languidly opened her eyes, blue like Basil's, when Lala came in, and asked that lady how she liked her new pug, with the ugliest, prettiest, little black and white face in the world, just as if they had met yesterday, instead of a year or so ago.

Lu Lu turned up her delightful little Japanese face to listen for the reply with an air of *naïveté* that would be simply delicious in a woman, and if found in the ladies of Lu Lu's country, possibly accounts for the extraordinary fascination exercised by Japanese ladies over English male minds.

"They call them Sleeve-dogs," went on the Princess plaintively, "but that's a mere trope —a mere figure of speech, and calculated to mislead one—anything and everything will go up a Chinaman's sleeve, you know, and Lu Lu is so very little!"

Lala discussed the beauty's points, and thought of Basil, who was so much less to his mother than the least of her long line of lap-dogs had ever been, then enquired for him, but found, as she expected, that his mother knew nothing of his whereabouts, and had not even heard of his latest diversion, whereupon Lala, with bistre marks under her grey eyes, and attired *à quatre épingles* as usual, told her, without comment, what had happened.

The Princess raised her eyebrows, delicate like Basil's, and smiled a little, with lips also delicate, and also like her son's.

"Such an inconvenient time of year," she said, "and he will miss all the best race meetings — a thing I never knew him do before. But I think I remember the girl. I haven't seen so much of him for years as I did last year—when he actually used to go to church that he might sit and look at her. I saw her once—quite a slip of a schoolgirl, with marvellous colouring, so vivid, yet so delicate—quite unique. Something like a cluster of exotics, you know—with a background of black velvet. He cooled off latterly, and I thought the matter at an end. I concluded she had been too eager, for that was Basil's way, what he could have easily, he would not take ; as a child we always gave him everything he wanted, because if we did not, he would go through fire and water to get it for himself. But his father and I have been really vexed with him lately—for we heard through our agents that he has been seriously impoverishing himself—he is rich, of course; he has all his uncle's money, you know, but fifty or sixty thousand pounds is a large sum to get rid of all at once—and he refused point blank to tell us where it had gone. Some lemon in your tea?"

Lala declined lemon, and the Princess, smoothing a fold of her grey velvet gown, continued to discourse of Basil.

"I wish he had been a girl," she said plaintively. "He is not much of a comfort. I'm sure he can't complain of the father I chose for him, as far as looks go—Strokoff was the handsomest man about the court at St. Petersburgh when I married him—and how was I to know he was going to turn out a Nihilist, and be exiled, and all the rest of it? It was at a ball at the White Palace I

met him first, and I wore——" and the Princess
slid off into recollections. "But I do hope
Basil does not mean to take up with his
father's nonsense—if the peasants would only
keep clear of the *kabák*, and not turn themselves into vodka bottles, they would not be
poor and miserable—the State would suffer of
course, but *they* would be all right."

Lala laughed. When her mouth curled up,
and her grey eyes shone, she was enchant-
ingly lovely, and the Princess looked at her
approvingly.

"I don't think you need—care," she said.

"No," said Lala. "Basil is just *a man*,
neither better nor worse. But it was stupid
of him not to leave orders about his team;
they're splendid brutes, and they've scarcely
been seen at a single meet this season."

"And I never go on a coach," murmured
the Princess; "so unbecoming, you know—
Venus herself would look a fright if perched
at such a height. But why don't you use

it? No one would know the coach without you on the box-seat. And Basil's disposition being what it is, I should say he will be back for the Derby—certainly for the Derby. If the—affair lasts till Ascot——" she paused, feeling her imagination unequal to the occasion.

"What a delightful gown you have on," said Lala, rising to go. "Mason? You will never do better. Good-bye. *Beaux regards* to the Prince."

"Let me know if you hear from Basil," said the Princess. "Good-bye. After all, I think your woman could give points to Mason . . . there is genius in that sleeve, and the woman who *can* cut a sleeve," and a tinge of colour came into her cheek, and she spoke with the solemnity befitting the theme, "you may trust blindfold."

It was the *dernier mot*. She sank back among her silken cushions, and closed her eyes, but was not destined to muse long on

the perfections of Lala's sleeves, which ought
surely to have kept Basil out of mischief—if
anything could, for from the garden entrance
a woman, wild-eyed, travel-stained and
terrible, made her way into that Paradise of
perfume and soft living, and told the Princess
some cruel truths.

"Your son has gone away with another
man's wife," said this woman, fierce as a
lioness robbed of her whelps, "and I helped
him. I loved her husband, and now I would
give my life blood, my soul hereafter, to give
her back to him. He would rather have her
ruined, disgraced than any other woman
pure. I must find her—because he is waiting
for her, and if he waits too long, he will go
mad. You bore Basil—you are his mother
and being a woman must help a fellow-woman
—you shall. Give me money—give it to me,
I say, or I will kill you with these hands—"
and she spread them out bare and scarred
before the terrified Princess, "these hands that

have already strangled one man, and can as easily strangle you."

The Princess looked, read murder in those eyes, quailed, and rose to do the criminal's bidding. No bell was within reach, the servants were at a distance, and in the depths of her shallow soul she knew that the stern demand was just, that her son had sinned, and that some one must pay the forfeit.

She sighed as she took from her escritoire a bundle of notes, they had been intended for her dressmaker, and Basil's sin assumed glaring colours as she viewed it through the glasses of a disappointed, and justly-incensed tradeswoman.

Hugon counted the notes swiftly, they amounted to just two hundred pounds.

"If I want more," she said, "I will come back," and with that comforting assurance, disappeared by the way she had entered, a door opening from the garden.

Lala sat very erect behind her black horses

going back to town, and on arriving there, bade the coachman drive to Prince Strokoff's rooms in Piccadilly. Her own servants, who knew, exchanged glances, but Basil's valet who had brought him up in the way that masters should go, stepped to the carriage with a perfectly expressionless face, and announced that the Prince had certainly arrived in town that forenoon, but left again for Paris almost immediately after.

" Alone ? " said Lala in a low tone, and with her most commanding glance.

The man remained silent, but looked at her in a way that she understood.

She nodded, and gave the order to drive home.

CHAPTER III.

" Hopes are among the living—the dead are beyond hope."
—Theocritus.

It was long before Nan even partially recovered from the horror of that night in which she had seen the abduction of her sister by Basil Strokoff. When she sped out of the gates in pursuit of the dog-cart, dropping her shoe as she went, and crying out wildly upon Easter to return, she had followed it as long as possible, and once felt sure she heard Easter calling back to her, and Basil speaking in angry tones, but soon the sound of wheels grew fainter, and when at last she reached the railway station for which she had instinctively felt they were bound, the yard was empty, the place all shut up, and she knew how slight was her chance of overtaking them now.

The rest of that night's adventures were

such as she was never able thoroughly to
recall, but the heroic little figure, half-clad,
with one shoe off, and one on, struggling
through the pitch darkness across country
with a dogged resolution to save Easter that
conquered all difficulties of time and place,
and terror of tramps, turned up at daybreak
many miles away, at a railway station not far
from Fitzwalters, and which had indeed been
erected for the special benefit of Bill and his
lively friends on their journeyings to and from
town.

It was Rufus himself who announced to
her that her quest was ended—in ruin, and
the station-master rudely wakened from his
slumbers was kind to the Meg Merrilies-like
child whose grief was a heart-breaking thing
to see and hear, as she made desperate
enquiry as to who had departed during the
night.

No tickets had been issued, as it happened,
nor had anyone been seen on the platform

before the one o'clock express came up, but some person or persons must have boarded the train at the last moment, for as the rear-end of it passed the station-master, he had banged to an open first-class carriage door, but had not time to see if any of the Fitzwalters people were inside it.

And then poor Nan, footsore, had got herself home, in a friendly market-gardener's cart as it afterwards transpired—and meeting Jem in the courtyard of Penroses, had with the quietness of absolute conviction told him the truth. She could not remember afterwards that he had said one word. Perhaps he did not.

I am sorry to say that Dinkie came out anything but well in this time of trial, as most unproven male things do. He was selfish of course—it is at once the privilege and glory of his sex—and one can handsomely say of him that he was not found wanting; if anything he exceeded his just allowance.

The average man mizzles when trouble comes to sit under his roof, and it is only the unhappy married one who is compelled to bear his fair share, and therefore, according to the legend, is exempted by St. Peter from suffering in the next world, though how about the poor upper servant wives? No such nice little arrangement seems to be made for *them.*

Dinkie then, found the domestic atmosphere so trying (for over and above other things, the money being Basil's, Tom enjoined a savage economy in all things), that he was seldom seen except at meal times, thereby increasing Nan's burdens, already sufficiently heavy. He was furious with Easter, and did not scruple to say so, while the thought of those flesh-pots, and other Hangingshaw delights from which her misconduct had cut him off, rankled unceasingly in his mind, which was of a greedy turn, as Nan in a burst of candour one day told him—poor Nan who dwindled and dwindled day by day till her

face looked almost ghost-like in its tangle of
red hair. Her idols lay broken in the dust,
and she could not reconstruct them, or take
pleasure in thinking of their beauty and
goodness any more. She was not even of any
use to her father, whose mood was too chafed
and stormy to be soothed to peace by a
woman-child's tender hand. And it was
strangely enough from without, that the first
gleam of consolation came, and from so
altogether unlikely a source as Daddy
Gardner.

He came over constantly, with commi-
seration running all down his long nose, and
they talked of Easter, usually in the wood-
house, a cool and commodious spot, sacred
to the storing of fuel, and chopping of logs,
in which it was Nan's custom to do most of
her thinking, and a great part of her suffering,
alone.

Sit in the warmth to feel, and in the cold
to think, and Nan's conclusions about the

world in general, and her own affairs in
particular, were mostly come to in this quiet
and unfrequented nook — unfrequented at
least in time of summer.

Daddy had no hard words or blame for
Easter, but turned purple over Basil's name,
and displayed an inveterate hatred to Hugon,
unusual in a man towards a friendless woman.
Easter had done no wrong—Easter was the
scapegoat for the pretty pair of villains' sins,
and gradually Nan's soul was raised from
contemplation of Easter in her degradation,
to the sister she had known, and curiously
fostered by Daddy, the timid hope grew and
strengthened in her that Easter was not
hopelessly dead to them — not hopelessly
wicked after all. She did not know how
the miracle of her rehabilitation was to be
performed, but while with Daddy all things
seemed possible, it was only when alone that
despair settled heavily upon her, that fathom-
less despair to which she had been a prey

long before Daddy found her one day, in the place where so many lonely hours had been spent, her head laid down on the battered old block, motionless and cold as ice with the exhaustion of grief. A sudden perception of how much suffering this young more or less uncared - for life had held, brought smarting tears to Daddy's eyes, and he half stretched out his hand to stroke that ruddy fleece of falling hair—for as a wise man has said, it is surely more reasonable that the old should weep than the young, while something was fighting in him for speech, it wrestled with him every time he saw Nan, but he thrust it back now as always, and whistled.

Then he sat down on a faggot near her, and in very recklessness of sympathy, as it seemed to her, began supposing this and that —supposing that Strokoff being such a brute, persuaded Easter away—and that they had repented, or *she* repented, before it was too

late, and he sent her back, having done no
wrong, after all?

"Then she would have come here," said
Nan, the big freckles on her pale face
standing out startlingly, "but he wouldn't
let her go. Basil was very reckless—it was
his great fault," added the child, who in spite
of everything and everybody, perhaps because
of everybody, as is the way with a faithful
friend, loved him still.

Daddy scrunched between his teeth some
nouns and adjectives with which he desig-
nated Basil's "recklessness," then enquired of
Nan if she had seen anything of Jem lately.

"Father won't let me go to the Shaw,"
replied Nan sadly, "and Jem has never set
· foot outside his gates since he went home,
and refuses to see anybody."

"I don't understand Burghersh," Daddy
burst out presently; "to sit down like a
paralytic and never attempt to find her—or
kill that beast—it's very beautiful and holy,

and whatever you like to call it, this sweet forgiveness, but if *I* were the woman run away with, I should be disgusted at my loss being taken in so Christian-like a spirit—and if I were the man, I'd *murder* the other one—or try to."

" He is sure that she will come home some day," said Nan, " and he is afraid to go away lest there should be no one to welcome her when she *does* come. O ! Daddy," the child burst out with tears in her voice, " he trusts her more than you or I do !"

" He is a fool," growled Daddy, " if he had scoured the place—" he stopped abruptly— " the world I mean, he must have found her by this. Easter isn't the sort to come whining to his gate like a beggar woman and crying : ' Peccavi ! ' Your father can't, and Burghersh won't, spend any money over the matter—a smart detective would have tracked out the whole thing ages ago—and cleared it all up."

For it was a long time ago as human

suffering goes, late spring had given way to summer, and Penroses was a feast of roses now; you could smell them through the open wood-house door, and the lusty summer song of countless birds mingled with their sad talk, and sometimes almost drowned it.

"Try and think it may all come right," said Daddy finally when he went away, leaving Nan to mourn over something more real than the ugliness and unlovedness over which she had wept so often here, for with Daddy's departure the sun had gone in, and she could not see how wrong could become right, or her idols be made whole and glorious to her again.

Daddy was always impressing upon her that nothing is irreparable but death—but had she thus lost both her dear ones she thought she could have borne it better than this. "Where the light is brightest, the shadows are deepest," and the shadows were at their very deepest about Nan then.

Late that night, Tom, turning impatiently from tobacco, lifted a corner of the green-room blind, and looked out into the night.

Something crossed the lawn—hovered like a wounded thing in the distance, then faded away.

"What was that?" cried the poor father with beating pulses, and dashed out in pursuit, but ghost, or shadow, or suffering human thing, whatever it might be, he could not find it—it was gone, but left its trace in startled nerves, and a desperate tug at his heart strings, as of some trouble close akin, and in very flesh and blood allied to his, behind it.

CHAPTER IV.

"How sickening, how dark the dreadful leisure
Of weary days, made deeper exquisite,
By a foreknowledge of unslumbrous nights . . .
And a whole world of lingering moments crept
Sluggishly by."

JEM stood gazing abroad at his kingdom which just then seemed intent, not on hanging its shaws (as its name signified), but on burying them.

The spirit of decay moved abroad unquietly, spotting the broad leaves of the sycamore, lightening the heavy oak boughs of their acorns, dimming the shining rind of the "lady of the woods," and turning her leaves to tawniest gold and amber; while the flowers that she suffered yet to scentless spring were with scarcely an exception yellow, after the fashion of Nature, who

has ever the right colours to suit her on
every possible occasion. Yellow too were
the pale leaves of the elm, now trembling
uncertainly to the ground as if doubtful of
their reception, and loath to leave the bough
where—through the long, happy summer,
each has been suffered to

"Dance as often as dance it can."

Ruddy were the bramble leaves that
clasped hands with the festoons of briony,
linking together the thickets of underwood
broken here and there with patches of golden-
blossomed furze, and yet more fragrant buck-
wheat, whose pungent odour recalls that of
birch trees in the dew of a spring early
morning, but a cold mist was stealing over
and blotting out all, and Jem shivered as
he stooped to pick a bit of heath flower
which he stuck in his coat, shifting his gun
from one arm to another as he did so. He
was never seen abroad without this gun,

which was his faithful companion when he
tramped mile after mile of country, till he
could tramp no more, having in a measure
transferred the pain of mind to his muscles,
and so ensured that lethargy of fatigue a
miserable human being falsely misnames rest.

It was well for him in these days that he
brought a right heart to Nature, or she could
not have comforted him as she did, for it is in
the heart of the man himself, that true
communion with her is established, and that
she proves herself warm friend, or harsh step-
mother. And to Jem, the wailing of the
autumn breeze through the pale woodlands
blended like a soothing voice with his
desolation, and a feeling of comradeship with
the lonely stone-chat who swings and swings
in the topmost bough in the wind on the hill;
the earth-scents that rose as grateful incense
to his nostrils, yea, the clouds, those
heavenly fleets ever hurrying on to a shore
whose glories we cannot see, but of which

they *know*, heartened and strengthened him to bear the agony that had been put upon him.

"For they can conquer who believe they can," and Jem, in those long months of endless days and nights, found that there are strong uses and blessings too, in sorrow, that to live with it—talk with it—sleep with it, to have no human being to whom you can transfer even a smallest portion of it—to rise above the wave, instead of being engulphed by it, means the finest discipline it is possible for a man to live through; and it is in such fiery trials as these that the real grit comes out, and the man himself is proven.

With Endymion might he well have said :

> " To sorrow
> I bade good-morrow,
> And thought to leave her far away behind ;
> But cheerly, cheerly,
> She loves me dearly,
> She is so constant to me and so kind ;
> I would deceive her,
> And so leave her,
> But ah ! she is so constant and so kind."

Open-eyed, conscious, with no human company to distract him, no excess to deaden, or anodyne to subtract one hour of waking pain, that man must be a strong one who holds fast to life and reason through so prolonged a crucifixion, and if Jem so far came out of it sane and alive, there were yet such signs and marks upon him as he would carry with him to his dying day.

He looked, spoke, and moved much as before, but the spontaneity of life—the healthy glow and stir of blood in his veins that give life and character to a man, had become frozen, and his complexion, for all his out-door existence, had become of the hue of parchment, while his shooting clothes hung upon his broad shoulders in sacks. The whole identity had withered outwardly, and yet, look at him which way you would, Jem was a *man*. If you had seen him among others—all dressed pretty much alike—he would not have taken precedence of any, for till the opportunity for testing his quality comes, you can't tell how any one of them will come off—but when the time for action does arrive, the real man or the tailor's dummy reveals himself, proved in action. And perhaps if Jem had known the height, and breadth, and depth of this calamity, with which he had set himself down to dwell, he would have turned, doubting and sickening from the task, but what he had begun in something akin to madness, he continued by sheer daily and hourly struggle to carry through, and even as the back is made for the burden, so must God's most awful decrees be carried out by us without fainting, or ever seeking to elude them.

Easter had gone away, but she would come back. To go and look for her meant that when she did return to the one faithful heart in the whole world that beat for her, she would mourn and believe herself cast off, perhaps shrink away to die, and he would

run no such risks. Of her, Jem thought
always as one without sin, but as an ab-
stract Easter, not the wife who had dwelled
beside him—rested in his arms—and who,
in her own wayward fashion, had surely
loved him.

If he had ever thought of her as a woman,
— loving, weeping, praying, sinning — his
calm would have been shattered, and he at
the mercy of his passions, but as a woman he
never did think of her now, while of Basil—
from *him* he was able by sheer force of
will to force his thoughts away, and, super-
human struggle though it was, he came off
as a rule, victor.

When he could control himself no longer—
when there threatened to rise in him that
awful lust to destroy *her* destroyer, that he
must never suffer to get beyond him, Jem
would rise up, and whether by night or day,
cover league upon league, never drawing
breath until he dropped half dead upon the

ground, and the devil for the time being, scourged out of him.

So many hours to tramp—so many hours to concentrate on books hard of digestion—so many hours devoted to matters connected with his estate, which he managed himself—a brief allowance of time for food, and then the slumber of exhaustion. Thus was his time parcelled out—thus did he fence himself from the demons of memory ever on his track.

The seasons mattered nothing, only like poor other humans, he felt his cross burn into him more deeply on fair days than on foul ones, and he would shut his eyes to the beauty he might not share with her he loved . . . thus they fought it out alone together, God and he — God to smite the blow, he to bear it, with nothing in earth or heaven to come between they two. Only, this afternoon, as he tramped through the long grass, and dead fern that clung round his ankles chillingly, coming at last to that glade that he never failed to visit once within each twenty-four hours, something, that was not hope, nor prescience, nor the dead peace of a worn-out spirit, but an intuition, life-giving and awakening, even as the wind that kindles with its breath all the fire and beauty of earth, came to him suddenly, so that standing still in the sodden wood, he suddenly threw back his shoulders as if a great weight had slipped from them, and baring his head, thanked God for he knew not what, only sure that somewhere—somehow, some good had come to him, and it must concern her he loved, and surely he would know it soon. He looked eagerly to right and left, as if he expected to see her stealing towards him through the silvery mist that now had risen about him, a gauze-like veil that a wizard might have woven to hide from him those joys that might kill him peradventure, did they reveal themselves

too suddenly to his ken . . . and so, with
gun resting on the ground, each nerve and
muscle strained to utmost tension, he stood,
waiting—feeling only the hammering of his
pulses and heart, sure as one is sure of death
—of life—that Easter, or news of her, was
close at hand, and that the long months of
his dreadful vigil were over.

For so it is, that one day God says, " It is
enough. This man has gone through all he
is able to bear ; he has borne it well. I will
set him back again in the sunshine," and He
wipes out the long agony, almost even the
memory of it, as if it had never been, though
through that anguish the man has been made
stable.

Jem had felt it coming . . . it was
there . . . and who but she should seek
him in this spot ? and sight and consciousness
nearly left him, when a woman's shape loomed
through that silver mist, and approached
him . . . a moment only he saw it, then

every instinct in his body told him that this was not Easter, and covering his face from sight of any other woman or thing, a groan of baulked longing burst from his heart, before which the figure fell away, becoming a mere dumb outline among the ghostly, dripping trees.

There came to him a low sound of weeping . . . of weeping . . . how dared this strange woman weep for *her?* . . a murderous impulse to point his gun at that contemptible, insignificant blur on the whiteness yonder, and wipe it out, shook him like a reed, and hunger, mad and clamorous for her he loved, tore at his heart like a vulture; his God had promised, then mocked him of His promise . . . and his cry rang out, *"Easter! Easter!"* voicing all the martyrdom of the past silent nights and days, and making the woman who heard it shudder, for was not this devil's work her own?

"Easter has sent you a message," said a

voice that trembled out of the mist, and Jem, striding forward, seized Hugon by the shoulders, and shook her violently, not knowing what he did. " Where is she? " he shouted.

" She is safe," said Hugon ; then when he realized what he was doing and had let her go—" and well," she added with a gasp. " So she bade me tell you."

"Thank God! Thank God ! "

He bared his head, looking upwards through the sodden leaves, all his torture forgotten, with the pathetic forgiveness of the beaten human child to its inscrutable Great Father. A little colour had come into his withered face, he was alive, and tasted the joy of living once more, the blood in his veins stirred, and the long midnight of his solitude was past.

" Take me to her," he seized Hugon's arm, and hurried her through the copse towards the house at such speed that she stumbled and almost fell over the uneven ground.

"You ask no questions," said Hugon, her face shewing spirit-like through the wreathing vapours. "How do you know that she is not with *him?*"

"She would have sent me no message then," he said, "and you"—he stopped to look at her, remembering what she really was—"you are a better woman than when I saw you last, or you would not bring it."

She looked pitifully up at him, and her mouth trembled. They were out of the wood now, and moving on level ground, and their faces were quite clear to one another, and there was death in hers, but he did not see it.

"Jem," she said, "before I tell you any more, will you tell me that you forgive me for all the wrong I have ever done you—and her?"

Jem shook his head.

"I've thought a good deal about it," he

said ; " I've had plenty of time for thinking, you know, this last six months, and I believe you led my poor little girl away between you —you and that scoundrel — and that for everything she has suffered, you are responsible. When you can prove to me that it isn't so, I'll forgive you, and not before."

They had come in sight of the Hangingshaw by now, the mists were rolling themselves grandly away up the cliff side, and in the red gleam of the autumn sun, the many windows of the house shone like beacon-fires, kindled as in welcome.

" She is not there," said Hugon, answering the devouring glance with which he swept the place, as if holding her, it must shout out aloud its joy to the whole world.

" Where is she ? " said Jem, stopping short and going white as ashes.

" I can take you to her within an hour."

He turned giddy, and leaned against the lintel of the door they were just entering,

and she thought he would have fallen, but
he recovered almost immediately, and they
passed into the house through the drawing-
rooms, where everything was just as when
Easter occupied them, flowers bloomed in the
jardinières, her work-box with its golden
thimble beside it stood open by her favourite
chair, drawn to the fire, no alteration or
neglect of any kind was visible in any part of
the place.

" My wife has gone away," he said to the
housekeeper on the occasion of her bringing
to him the key of Easter's jewel safe, and
wardrobes. " When she comes back I wish
her to find everything just as she left it," and
that was the first and last time he ever spoke
on the subject of his wife to any person of
his household, or out of it.

The same hours were kept, the same rooms
prepared, the only difference being that when
in the house he habitually used his study,
as the table piled with dry-as-dust books

abundantly testified. No flowers were here, but Easter's portrait, enlarged from an old photograph, taken when she was sixteen, was placed where it must always catch his eye, and every gleam of sunshine that entered.

"Good morrow to thee, my darling," he murmured tenderly to it now as he came in. " I never pass her without speaking," he added abruptly to Hugon, "night and morning, and often between, I talk to my little girl, and she smiles back at me—don't you see her smiling now ? " And indeed the girlish face seemed to answer him with its innocently gay mirth.

But Hugon had bowed her head, and was weeping those tears—tears of repentance— that are the most grateful tribute to God that a human soul can offer.

Jem's face changed and an unutterable dread swept across it.

" You're not hiding anything from me," he said. " She is not ill—dying ? "

Hugon looked up, her face touched with

42*

that greater glory which is not of earth, and which only those within measurable distance of the hills of heaven ever wear.

"All is well with Easter," she said, then below her breath, "and with you. She must tell you herself . . . come."

CHAPTER V.

Daddy that same afternoon tore into the wood-house, now very cold, not to say mildewy in its melancholy, snatched up Nan who was writing poetry on the much-scarred block of wood to which so many cheerful logs had fallen, and careered with her round and round the place, at the same time uttering whoops that might have alarmed a person who did not recognise them for what they were—manifestations of the purest and most irrepressible joy.

" *Easter !* " shrieked out Nan, wildly excited, when at last he set her down and, " Easter it is ! " he responded in ecstasy, then, without pausing to take breath, began to dance a jig like one possessed.

"Dance!" he cried, "dance! O! you'll *dance* now for the rest of your days! No more sackcloth and ashes—no more howls and red noses—don't ask me to explain, only dance, shriek, rejoice! I've got good news, splendid news, rare news, and I must let off some of the steam a bit, or I shall burst!"

And Nan danced, for it was one of her doubtful accomplishments that she could dance a jig—with all her heart, and soul, and body, and with eyes alight, and arms akimbo did a double shuffle in such style as quite to cut out Daddy's performance, whooped twice to his once, displaying a perfect genius for savage and warlike yells that he toiled after in vain, and found herself dancing on her own cherished poetry, rhyming from top to bottom with death and sorrow, shame and blame, and danced on it all the harder; then when she had to stop because her stockings had come down altogether, and enveloped her shoes, wound up by rushing into Daddy's arms where they rocked to and fro, patting each other's backs encouragingly, and inarticulately gurgling out new forms of satisfaction as they tried to recover their breath, and impart and receive information at the same moment.

" I don't know what it's all about—but I *know* it's all right," said Nan, just as Dinkie's chilly voice was heard enquiring if this were Pandemonium let loose, or had his refined and accomplished sister *at last* gone off her blooming chump?

"Stow that," growled Daddy, still out of breath, " and run and get your hat, Nan— you've got to go somewhere with me—you know who it is to see—directly. The dog-cart's waiting outside the kitchen garden."

Nan jumped clean up into the air—I should be sorry to say how many feet she jumped— but I am sure she could never do it again

as long as she lived — and gave one final
whoop of such surprising power and intensity
as to nearly crack Dinkie's ears, and scatter
all the fowls in the near neighbourhood, tore
once round the circumscribed limits of the
wood-house with headlong joy, and vanished.

" What is it all about ? " said Dinkie, who,
to use one of his own expressions, was never
so unterconstumbled in his life.

" O ! you'll hear in good time," said Daddy,
who by no means approved of Dinkie's eternal
selfishness to Nan, and when she herself
appeared in a jiffy, having covered herself with
a long cloak that trailed the ground, and
capped it with an extremely dirty sun-bonnet,
Dinkie could not get anything out of her
either, though her manner of snubbing him
raised an agony of curiosity in his breast.

" You haven't been a bit nice about Easter,
Dinkie," she said, draping the Ancient
Mariner's old cloak in toga fashion about her,
and feeling indeed that it was a suitable

garment in which to administer rebuke to her elders ; "it wasn't *her* you missed or cared about—or felt *sorry* for—but the tuck-outs and tips and things—for you always were a greedy, and now you know it."

Having touched her mentor up on this his sorest point, it was a pity that in turning away with uncommon dignity to make a stately exit, Nan should have been tripped up by the folds of her cloak in such wise as to precipitate her head first into Dinkie's stomach, and being thence ejected with great vigour and promptitude, rebounded on to the adjacent pile of faggots, out of which (being swathed like a mummy in its wrappings) Daddy presently, and with much laughter, fished her.

It cannot be denied that this accident somewhat moderated Nan's overflowing spirits and even affected her manners, for it is a fact that when she was re-adjusted, and Dinkie spitefully drew her attention to what he

called her "rotten effusions" on the ground,
she deliberately said, "*Blow* it!" and walked
out with a stately swagger.

But when Daddy had tucked her into the
dog-cart that was lying *perdu* in a convenient
spot (Dinkie loftily viewing the proceedings
from a distance) and had taken his place
beside her, it was a subdued Nan, all her wild
tumult of joy over, who looked up eagerly
into Daddy's face.

"What did I always tell you?" he said
with the air of an earthly Providence as they
turned off the grass into one of the cart-ways
that led from Penroses to the town, "that if
you'd only keep up your pecker, things might
come right in the end? Well, they *have* come
right — everything's come right — even that
Satan in petticoats, Hugon, ain't so bad after
all—and we're just going to have a good
time all round, and more especially Jem
Burghersh. Not but what I blame him," he
added, a touch of sternness in his young face,

" she had only a fancy for the other fellow and he should have squashed it, but he let him come fooling round in town, and then he leaves her here alone, and he has himself to thank for everything—for if a man can't look after his own wife, who will? But he's had a pretty rough time of it—poor chap—he must be there by now," and Daddy looked at his watch; " by Jove, that Shaker business of ours took longer than I thought," and he put his pony along at a great pace.

" Where are we going?" cried Nan as they left the town behind, and the trees and hedgerows spun past, "this is the way to Minsterton ! "

" And to Minsterton we're going," said Daddy with a grin that pastured on his nose and mouth indefinitely. " O ! you won't think me such a fool when you know all the ins and outs of everything ! But I'm not going to tell you anything—not till you've seen her—so it's no good trying your blandishments upon *me*."

"Jem," said Nan in a trembling voice almost lost in the depths of a turned-away sun-bonnet, "where is . . . *he?*"

Poor Nan had heard her sister called by many a straight and brutal name during these past months, and if such terms of shame had not been applied to Basil also, it was because though a man may and does, sin often, there is no such word as shame for him in the vocabulary.

"Well," said Daddy cheerfully, "she is not alone, if you must know, and most extraordinarily attached to that person she is, in fact won't let him out of her sight, though *I* can't see anything in him myself——"

He stopped, frightened at the silence inside the sun - bonnet, and peeping inside, saw Nan's small face at the other end, drowned in tears.

"It's a blackguardly shame," he exclaimed, greatly moved, "dear, dear little Nan, you're all wrong—do you think I should take you there if—if—but here we are," and he drove smartly in at the gates of his home.

Minsterton was barely a half mile out of the town, but it might have been a hundred away from the clash of the machinery, the loud voices of the factory hands, and the more or less bustling life of Rokehorn, upon which it turned its back, and, lying at some distance from the highway, was approached by a privet-bordered road that led only to the Manor House, the churchyard, and, close beside the latter, Minsterton itself.

Side by side stood the little gate which gave entrance to a paved walk, sentinelled with giant yews, to the bigger one that led through a short shrubbery to a square gravelled court upon which looked picturesque stables, their high, narrow windows framed in now scarlet Virginia creepers, to a long, low, many-windowed house, magnolia-leaved, and in summer, starred with heavy fragrant cups, while on the third side, the back of a grey church with its dead nestled itself lovingly in close to the living, with only a high laurel hedge to divide them.

Unutterably peaceful was the atmosphere of the whole place, more especially on the south side, where from the sunny verandah, about whose twisted pilasters in summer, roses clung, one looked over lawn and park-like field that merged themselves imperceptibly into swelling hills, crowned in one place by ancient cedars that looked down on a green altar where many sacrifices were said to have been consummated, and to which, from time immemorial, had been given the name of Baals.

The little church at the side, the old-world air of it all, the struggle of life going on out of sight, out of earshot, made one feel instinctively that here might either the very young, or the very old find happiness indeed, and tears came into Nan's eyes at its beauty, for she knew that inside that porch-like door she would find Easter.

"Daddy," she cried breathlessly, a sudden light breaking in on her, "you have known it all along . . . that was why you tried to comfort me . . . she has been here . . . almost at our very gates . . . and you never told me . . . O! it was cruel, *cruel* of you!"

"Couldn't," said Daddy briefly. "You'd have told Dinkie, and he'd have told Jem—there's only one way of ensuring your neighbour holding his tongue, and that is by holding your own. I see by the way the gravel's cut up he is here already, and I'd given my oath not to speak, so had mother. But ticklish work it was when I was with you, I promise you," added Daddy, as he beckoned a distant gardener, and got out, helping down Nan, who, between the awkwardness of her cloak, and the trembling of her limbs, was an uncertain quantity to lay hold of.

They met no one as they crossed the quiet

old hall, with its low window seat full of those flowers that seem always to bloom best without air, and behind glass, but they saw in the distance a stout, matronly person in a cotton gown who brought some vague reminiscence to Nan's mind. Surely she had seen some such person not once, but many times, at Penroses. . .

"Why are you taking me upstairs?" she cried wildly, "is she ill?"

"No, not exactly ill. You'd better go in alone." He opened a bedroom door a very little way, pushed Nan and her cloak inside it, then drawing a deep breath as he shut it behind her, listened.

A smile broke over his face, then he winked violently to get rid of some moisture in his eyes as he went downstairs.

"God bless Nan!" he said.

CHAPTER VI.

" Ye who have yearned
With too much passion, will here stay and pity
For the mere sake of truth."

"WHAT is the doctor doing here ? " Jem had enquired fiercely half-an-hour earlier, as Hugon led him up the stairway, and pausing on a certain threshold had rested awhile with averted head, and hand pressed hard against her side.

He did not see her face as she softly opened the door, and made a sign to him to enter, nor yet Mrs. Gardner, who rose on his entrance and quietly passed out . . . he saw only with a rush of longing that winged his feet to her, Easter lifting herself among her pillows, ethereal, purified, holding out eager arms to him, and when he was within them, looking deep, deep into his eyes as no

sinful woman surely ever looked at her true
lover yet, and so drew his head down to her
breast, and held it there with murmured
words of blessing, of love, of prayers for
forgiveness.   .   .   .

Forgiveness! The word stung him out of
his paradise. Why had she uttered it? He
moved restlessly in that close embrace, and
kneeling beside the bed, looked up in agony
in her face.

"My boy," she said pitifully, "my poor,
poor boy   .   .   ." then haltingly as one
afraid, passed her hand over the hollows in
his cheeks and temples, and touched the deep
lines she had drawn on his forehead, then
pressed her mouth to them, lingeringly,
hungrily, as if his very blemishes were
passionately dear and beautiful in her eyes.
And still he looked at her, not dazed, for
every touch was healing to him, only he who
had known so much sorrow was not fit to
bear joy—till she came to his lips, then

taking his head between her two hands, offered him all her sweet face and said: " Won't you kiss me, dear ? "

He shivered, his breast rising and falling in quick pants, yet with something in his eyes that pierced and thrilled her too, for so might look an angel who made question of a human soul, who might forgive indeed, but must and would know all the truth . . . and right across that unanswered question came a little cry that caused Jem to start up trembling, as Easter, with a glorious look of happiness, turned down the coverlid beside her, and lifted a little bundle that she first regarded with the most intense pride, then held out to him as if it represented all the treasure and loveliness of the whole world.

" Jem," she said—and where had she learned that voice of love ?—" our child . . ." and she laid him in his father's arms.

43*

The thrill of that baby-touch would have given him back his manhood even if he had lost it, but he had not, and only the pure rapture of his fatherhood came to him then . . . there was much to know, to explain, but he looked from the child to his mother, from the mother to her child—and believed her.

"Jem," she said, and her voice ran on like a babbling brook that for very joy must babble, and knows not how to stop, "he has grey eyes, just like yours, and *no* dimple in his chin like wicked me, so he is sure to grow up good like you—and as I mean to be, Jem, O! as I mean to be, dear! She has told you all about it of course . . . and you know how bad I was, but not so bad as you thought . . . and it was not Hugon's fault, she gave me a downward push—yes —but the wickedness was *here* in my heart, and it's all out now—but O! it's left a scar, Jem, it's left a scar!" and she broke out into

wild weeping that startled the babe from its
slumber, and she checked it, that she might
take him in her arms and soothe him. " But
I wanted discipline and I got it--and you did
not want it, but you got it too.   And you had
nobody, poor, proud, lonely boy, but I would
not, dared not—come, till I had—this."

She drew the soft little head closer with one
arm, the other was round Jem's shoulders and
his hidden face, as he kneeled beside the pair.

" And I had Hugon . . . . and we
talked of you—always of you—if I had not
been with someone who really loved you,
understood you, I think I should have died—
she spoke of you from the heart, not the lips
—and knew your goodness through and
through.   But, O ! it was hard to keep away
from you . . . . all alone there, my
dear, brave, lonely Jem, keeping your house
open for a poor, guilty wretch such as you
thought me, to creep into as a refuge at
last. . . ."

"*As he thought her.*" . . . what was it that she had *not* done, that Hugon had neglected to tell him. . . . slowly he lifted his head and looked at her, this was Easter, his own pure wife . . . the rest was a fable. . . . he reached up thirstily to her lips, drawing mother and sleeping child into his strong arms, and asked no more. . . . It was thus that Nan found them when, trembling with emotion, she stole across the room—and sinking down beside them, burst into a passionate flood of excited tears that seemed as though they would never stop.

"Dear Nan — brave Nan," said Easter, laying her frail hand on the child's glorious fleece of hair. "Don't forget, Jem, that it was Nan who really saved me that night . . . . that I might have gone with him —may God forgive me!—but for Nan."

"O! *Easter!*" cried the child, in a loud, awakened voice, and leaping up, "then you

did not go with him after all . . . .
Thank God! thank God!" and careered
around like mad till a certain sick-room
atmosphere suddenly struck her, and she
came soberly back to the bed beside which
Jem was now sitting, asking himself how many
hours ago he was tramping alone through the
sodden woods . . . . *she had not gone
away with Basil at all* . . . .

"But you have been very cruel, Easter,"
said the child, reproachfully, not having seen
that mystery over which Easter had drawn
the silk coverlid, " you might have trusted
me . . and Jem. . ."

For a moment Easter's face became wan,
and she fell back among the cushions wearily,
as one all too used to sorrow.

" Do you think I have been playing while
you wept?" she said. " Ask Hugon—ask
Daddy—and his mother, the best friend
surely, a wicked girl ever had, if I did not
grieve about you—I used to steal out after

dark, and go round by the fields and look in at Penroses—at poor father—once he nearly caught me—O! poor father, and poor mother, too . . . and I have stood under your window, Nan, where you think your strange thoughts . . . and I longed to call to you . . . but I dared not . . . not till baby came; I thought perhaps everybody might forgive me then . . . but I broke up the home, I tortured all your hearts —and Jem—look at the hollows in his face," and she looked earnestly, pitifully, at her work. "I can never undo it all—never," she added, with tears, as he stooped and kissed her hand as if she were a saint.

"O! the *dear* little thing!" screamed out Nan, starting back as the coverlid fell aside, and she saw the tiny creature tucked in to his mother's side. "Is it—is it——" then, as the wonderful truth dawned upon her, she fairly broke down and sobbed aloud, then hugged the pair of them till she woke the baby up, and entreated to be allowed to hold him.

"Isn't he heavy?" said Easter, with sparkling eyes — a radiant young mother whose face now had the last and crowning touch to its loveliness. "It's so funny for it to be so precious, considering how we grumbled at the babies at Penroses!"

"*I* didn't," said Nan indignantly, who had indeed nursed and dropped Maria's babies till it was a miracle they all grew up without blemish, "I *always* loved them!" And she retired with her prize to a distant window of that large and pleasant room that overlooked the garden, and the swelling hills beyond.

"And I love him most, Jem, because he is yours," said Easter, as she leaned her head against his breast.

"Little mother!" said Jem, smoothing her dark head with gentle hungry hand, as if he could never satisfy himself with touch of her. "And why was I not sent for sooner?"

"It was all arranged, dear, that if I showed signs of going to a wicked place—O! but I've got my punishment *here*," she broke off abruptly, with a cry of pain in her voice, "I believe we all do if we only knew it—that hell is just another name for conscience, and we're all punished just in the way that hurts us most! It was my pride, my stiff-necked pride, that had to be broken—and God broke it, Jem, broke it all into little pieces, and I don't mean ever to try and put it together again! Basil didn't love me," she added, looking steadfastly up at Jem. "I must speak of him just this once to you, dear—and then it will be over! That was the worst of it—if he had really loved me—if I had roused any truest part of him—but it was not *me*—not my heart, or soul, or the best that was in me —it was just a caprice he had been provoked into, and I hated Lala Hoyos—do you remember when I said it would be pull devil, pull baker, between us? Don't take your

hand away from my head, Jem . . . . .
I've only had one thought, one desire, to
creep back to the haven that once sheltered
me, to fold my arms round your neck, and
rest upon your strength as I always did without knowing it, to feel the arms of my true
love round me once again. . ."

He stooped down and kissed her hair . . .
she was so grandly justifying his belief in her
all the way along, and the constancy of her
nature, bound to outlast, in the long run,
any passing whim, was no surprise to the
man who had loved and trusted her to the
verge of folly—ay, to the bringing down upon
him of the world's huge contempt.

For, though she had in one passive moment
—a moment for which she could never clearly
account—almost thrown away home, love, and
character, yet, having done it, she had somehow found strength to stand up against the
inevitable consequences, and her real grit and
strength of principle had asserted itself. And

even of her might have been written Browning's exquisite lines :

> " For you could not, sweet!
> We might pray you, flay you, bray you
> In a mortar—but you could not, sweet."

" Jem," she said, wonderingly, " how does love grow? It is like looking one day for strawberries, and when you lift the leaves only green sides are there—you look again, perhaps the very next day, and you find the ground covered with scarlet fruit, almost over-ripe . . . and there are more than you can eat—only I don't love you a bit more than I know what to do with, dear. But if I had gone back to you—fresh from that awful night in which I was unfaithful to you—in heart, if not in deed—I should not have purged my sin . . . and I might have been grateful, but I should not have *loved* you then as now—now that you have proved yourself and your faith in me . . . you who have stood up, and taken the brunt

of it all . . . but I have suffered, Jem—
O! I have suffered! I loathed myself as
something unclean, fit neither to live nor die "
—she clung to him weeping—" but God and
Hugon were good to me through it all—and
you never saw a prettier, *bigger* baby, did
you? "

Jem kissed the lovely transparent face,
knowing that at last, and there was no question about it, through bitterest teaching, his
wife had learned that lesson of love at which
she had been so inapt and unwilling a pupil
always.

" They call that field over there, Baals,"
she said, dreamily looking out through the
distant window. " Day after day I have lain
here, and looked at it . . . and I have
laid my sacrifices there too, Jem, like the
Druids . . . and I used to ask Daddy if
he were *sure* you would accept it, and he
always said ' Yes,' you know a man always
says something kind."

"And he was right," said Jem, who himself, gaunt, hollow-eyed, looked like some young monk fresh from endless days and nights of self-maceration, yet with all the strength and passion of a man's nature unbroken in him yet, and resolute to follow a man's life to the end.

"They have been so good to me," she went on, "Daddy and his mother . . . I could never make it up to them . . . I can only cry over them, and *love* them all my life."

"Daddy is a dear," said Nan, who, approaching with her precious bundle, heard the last words, and suddenly remembering their saltatory feats in the wood-house, and Dinkie's outraged sensibilities thereat, was seized with a sudden fit of laughter, but in the midst of it thought of others not so happy as herself, and first her heart flew to her father, then to Hugon, the message of whose face had been read by her clearly enough, though in the absorption of the interview with Easter, she had until now forgotten it.

" Poor Hugon looks very ill," she said, shaking her head sadly, even while she thrilled with joy as the baby's hand froze on to one of her thin fingers, " and did she come to you *here*, Easter, when she ran away from Penroses ? "

" You'll know it all some day, Nan," said Easter, turning her ethereal white and rose face on the child. " It's a long story . . . but whatever wrong she may have done me once, she has amply atoned for it since. But for her, though the Gardners were so good, I don't think I could have lived through these awful six months—only she won't touch my baby, Jem—*our* baby, I mean. I know she loves it, for she sits looking at him for hours —and it's she who finds out all the little things in which he is like you—but she won't take him in her arms, and puts them behind her if I try to make her, though the tears

stream down her face for longing all the
while."

Jem did not seem to be attending—but he
was thinking hard, as he drew his wife's hand
softly across his lips.   Hugon would not
touch the little innocent child because blood
was on her hands . . .   yet surely she
had atoned . . .   she had washed them
clean in her repentance . . .   and Easter
did not know . . .   never need know
. . .   he thanked Hugon from his soul for
having found strength and spared her—to God
and him she had confessed her sin—it was
enough.

"I'll go and fetch her," he said, and lingeringly, as one who feared to put himself too
far from his treasure, he left the room to seek
her.

Nan came over and kneeled down by her
sister, and the two faces, curiously alike at
that moment for all their diverseness, both
illumined by an inward beauty now, looked

long and lovingly into each other, giving question and answer both.

" Kiss me, Nan," said Easter. " Why did you waken that night but to save me ? For I left you fast asleep."

" Why did you come to me ? " said Nan earnestly, " but that God sent you ? You did not mean to go away with him—or you would not have come to me."

" No," cried Easter, in ringing tones, " I had no thought of going . . . I was running away *from* him, not with him. . . . I would not trust myself to see him again . . . God knows how I got away from him in the drawing room that night . . . it was by the skin of my teeth . . . but I did . . . and I waited till all the house was asleep . . . I had often harnessed Rufus before, and I could do it again, and go home to the Shaw, and wait there for Jem . . . and Basil must have been hidden in the house, and followed me . . . and he

let me put Rufus in the cart . . . the
lanthorn shewed me, though I could not see
him, and just as I was going to start, he
stepped out of the darkness, and . . . it
all began over again. . . . Oh! Nan, it
was not love, not love, but a mad, bad, brutal
passion . . . and yet he swayed, he
possessed me . . . love had called me
once, and I would not go . . . and now
something that was not love beckoned me,
and I was intoxicated, for the time at least
he had mastered me . . . I might have
gone . . . I might have gone . . .
and then you came, and he thrust you aside,
oh! poor Nan! but the thrust fell on my
bare heart, and he leaped into the cart and
drove furiously away, but I heard you calling,
calling, long after your voice must have ceased,
and it made me broad awake, and I saw what I
was doing, what he wanted me to do, clear as
day . . . and you had saved me, Nan,
though you did not know it. ' Put me

down!' I said, and when he would not, but drove faster, and the cart rocked to and fro in the ruts, I tried to throw myself out, but he gripped me like a vice and said, 'By God, Easter, if you do, I'll drive over your body— dead or alive, I've got you, and I'll keep you too,' and so we zigzagged on, for Rufus had bolted, till at last, close to the Fitzwalters station, something snapped with a crash, and we were both thrown out into the road.

"When I came to myself, he was calling me by every mad and foolish name of love, but I would not listen, and then he grew angry again—and next happened the most wonderful, the most incredible thing—we heard wheels approaching, and who should it be, driving all alone, but Daddy! I saw his face clearly by the lamps, and when he saw the smashed dog-cart and Basil, and asked what was the matter, Basil flew at him, and in the midst of their quarrelling, I jumped into the cart, seized the reins, and drove away. There's a lot more to tell you—how he brought me here—how he hid me—of the brick he has been to me—but there isn't time now. . ."

Jem came in at that moment, leading Hugon. There were marks of tears upon her face, which was yet peaceful, as one over which the last storm has passed—now comes rest. She stooped down to kiss Easter, and Jem, looking earnestly at her, and in a way that she understood, laid his young son gently in her arms.

CHAPTER VII.

"It is well worth while to learn how to win the heart
of a man the right way. Force is of no use to make or
preserve a friend, who is an animal never caught and
tamed but by kindness and pleasure."

DADDY's subsequent relation of the events
that occurred on a certain remarkable night
in spring, took place in the usual *rendezvous*,
the wood-house, and was so interesting as to
make both him and Nan forget the cold,
though their blue noses—the more especially
Daddy's, which was always a splendid adver-
tising medium—attested to the severity of the
weather without doors, for all the summer
satisfaction that might reign their hearts
within.

Daddy indeed had been somewhat exercised
in his mind how to Bowdlerise his version of

things so as to meet the requirements of this
child who apprehended every variety of good
so easily (even finding it when it did not
exist), but had so very little practical knowledge of evil in any of its branches. He
finally compounded the matter by those
pungent little asides to himself duly set
down below, while his communications to
her were as strictly orthodox as his vocabulary, and liberal turn of thought allowed.

"Well," he said, "I had been out to
supper, you know, and I was driving home
(awfully sprung), when I found myself going
slap into a sort of picnic in a lane—at least
there was the Muscovite walking delicately
about like Agag among the ruins of a trap,
Rufus munching grass in a ditch, and Easter
—well, I didn't see her as I pulled up, and enquired politely what he was doing there—
('What the devil are you up to *now*?' I said),
and he replied with equal politeness (he told
me to go to hell), that that was *his* business.

I'd always been a sort of buffer between him and Easter, and he loved me properly for it —you bet—and then I got a turn, for Easter hopped out of the hedge, like an india-rubber ball, climbed into the trap, and snatching the reins out of my hands—awful bad form that —quite inexcusable—started off the Boss at express speed, and before Strokoff could stop her. He'd have pulled her out of the cart if she hadn't been quicker than greased lightning, for the lamp-light flashed on his face, and of all the demons I ever saw—like a burglar when his pal makes off with the swag —and we always thought him such a well-bred chap too ! When we'd gone a bit of a way, and I'd got my breath back, ' Daddy,' she said, ' it isn't every wicked girl who's got *one* guardian angel to watch over her—and I've got two—you and Nan ! ' I thought this pretty good for a beast like me—(but she'd frightened me sober)—and her face was white as chalk when she turned it round on me.

And though she had often been angry with me before, I knew she wasn't now.

" 'Daddy,' she said, 'you warned me only a few days ago—and I was very rude to you —all the same you made me promise if ever I were in trouble I'd come to you—and you'd help me—well, I want you to redeem that promise now. Only first you must swear me an oath that you will do just what I want— and that you will never tell a living soul what that is, till I give you leave.' Well, you know, Nan, it was rather a large order, and I hesitated a bit, and she blazed out at me like a million Gatling guns all going at once, and 'I was mistaken in you,' she said, all of a sputter, like girls in a rage. 'Stop the cart— *I'm* going to get out.' 'And *I'm* going to drive you home,' I said, feeling riled, 'and I won't go,' she flashed out, 'not to Penroses, nor to the Hangingshaw—I'm not fit to go to either—I'll kill myself first.' ('Jerusalem!' I thought, 'it's too late for anyone to do any-

thing now '), but when we came to the cross
roads, she sent the Boss flying along the road
to Minsterton, and as if she meant it too.

"'Are you coming home with me?' I said,
fairly taken aback. It's awkward when a
beautiful young woman drops in to tea with
you at two o'clock in the morning, and in the
bosom of your family too.

"'Daddy,' she said, looking up in my face,
and you know what Easter's coaxing ways
can be when she likes, 'are you going to
swear that oath to me, or are you not? Of
course you can go back upon your word if
you like—but if you don't, things may come
right yet.' Daddy paused to whistle. "Well
—Nan, it was a desperate young voice, and
a desperate young face, and I swore what she
wanted, and a devil of a time I've had of it
since, but when you're as fond of her as I
am—" he gulped down something hard, and
went on with his story.

"'Very well, then,' she said, quite pleased

when she'd made a big fool of me—excuse me,
Nan, but if I hadn't been one I shouldn't have
done it—you'd never catch an old married
man on the hop like that—' and now you've
got to hide me away somewhere that Jem, and
father, and everybody can't find me—I've got
plenty of money in my pocket, poor Jem's
money, you know.'

" 'It's all rubbish,' I said, knowing what a
fearful blunder she was making, and hating
to aid and abet it, ' probably no one even
knows you've left Penroses—and you can
easily slip in'—and then I thought of Rufus,
and the bits of the dog-cart—(and women
always leave a letter behind to explain the un-
explainable), and saw things might be awkward, and I stuck fast.

" 'I won't go back,' said Easter, setting her
little teeth like a spring, and she stopped the
Boss in the middle of the road to argue it out,
and we were no nearer at the end of half an
hour at coming to a decision than when

we began. She seemed possessed by a
horror of herself (as something vile—and this
upset me—she knew so much more what
she'd been up to than I did) she *could* not,
would not, go back to either house, 'and if
you attempt to carry me there—' she said, ' I'll
kill myself,' which you'll admit was mean,
and playing it rather low down on her
guardian angel and calculated to make him
wish he'd stayed up top. I didn't know of
course how far—" here Daddy coughed and
interrupted himself, feeling that asides were
dangerous indulgences, " but anyway the only
thing that came into my head at last was to
take her home to Minsterton, for the present
at all events," and Daddy pulled up his collar,
" for Mother's one of the good old-fashioned
sort that respects a man, and always does
what I tell her. And we're awfully quiet,
you know (at least Mother is), and if a place
lies off the market road, it may as well be a
hundred miles from civilization—no one

bothers about it—and our servants are old ones—and had never seen Easter—*they* wouldn't peach, still I had the jim-jams pretty bad when we drove up to the door, and thought of the hue and cry after her, and what lies I should have to tell—though if I'd known what it would cost me to tell them to *you*, Nan, I'd have seen my oath further first. Well, only Mother was up, and I just asked her to make Easter comfortable, then took the dog-cart round, and what the women said to each other I don't know—only Mother took it all right, and seemed to understand, as I'm jiggered if I could, and next morning never attempted to make Easter go home and do her duty—said she was ill—O! there are women's reasons for everything—and Easter just bewitched her as she does everybody else, and Hannah and Martha were her slaves too —and horses wouldn't have drawn a word out of any one of them. Mother soon found out the rights of everything, and had her own

reasons for not thinking it wise to force
Easter back to Jem, feeling as Easter did
about it, that she couldn't ask him to forgive
her till—till the little beggar came—O! Lord!
she wanted me to hold him the other day,"
and he squirmed all over at the thought—
"just to see how heavy it was! But it cut
me up to see you all going about two
double with grief for what hadn't happened,
and that a word from me could have put
right, and I was like the parrot when the
monkey picked off all his feathers—I had a
hell of a time."

"But *she* suffered too, poor Easter," said
Nan wistfully. "It's a different face now
altogether."

"Yes," said Daddy, looking away, "she
suffered, and no mistake—and it was Jem—
always Jem, when it wasn't those at home. I
believe she had been in love with him the
whole time she thought herself in love with
Basil, and so, what with thinking of him, and

sneaking over with me after dark to Penroses, and making the little beggar's clothes, and pottering about the garden (she actually tried to learn gardening to please the Chief), she got through the time somehow, and Hugon helped her a lot. Hugon was so fond of Jem too, you know," added Daddy with a queer look in his eyes.

"Did she come to you when she left Penroses?" said Nan, a look of sorrow crossing her bright face.

"No—not till June. She gave me a turn, I can tell you, when she walked in and asked for Easter. That brute Strokoff had told her he left Easter with me, when she ran him to earth at last, so she came here direct."

"Poor Basil," said Nan, softly. "If Easter has repented bitterly, so has he. He is very reckless, and he was angry with her, and all the worst in him came out." ("I should rather think it did!" murmured Daddy in

one of his asides.) " But I'm sure he is *my*
Basil again, long before this."

" Well," said Daddy with considerable dis·
pleasure, " I didn't know before that Penroses
was exactly a hatching ground for saints. To
upset the whole apple-cart, as the Muscovite
did (a beast I call him), and then to be *pitied!* "

" O ! we are all wicked sometimes," said
Nan sadly, " and I should think a person
without any faults would be perfectly ghastly
to live with ! Just think how he would be
able to disimprove every occasion, and preach
at you ! The only really *nice* good people I
ever knew are old—without enough go in
them to be wicked—or have a real bust-up.
But if you turned over the back pages in
their lives, you'd find *they'd* done some wrong
things too, in their youth ! And I can't be
angry with anybody, Daddy, I'm too happy.
There's father—he looks ten years younger
already. He hated so to think Basil a
scoundrel——"

"Which he is," interpolated Daddy viciously.

"And poor mother has actually looked out a pink bonnet. She's been wearing bottle-green ones all the summer!"

"But Mr. Denison'll never forgive us," said Daddy, with conviction, " not any single one of the blooming lot of us—Quixotic asses—Colney Hatchites—treacherous toads, he calls us, beginning with Easter, and including the family doctor, who knows all your constitutions, and knew where Easter was too — the poor old fellow has been trembling for his skin all round, ha! ha!— and ending with your humble servant—more especially your humble servant — and the Chief didn't exactly illuminate his conversation with texts, when he came over to Minsterton. Even the Mater came in for some of it, but he didn't get much change out of her, for I heard it all, and patted her on the back afterwards for the way she spoke up.

" ' Mr. Denison,' she said in her quiet way, ' to have forced your daughter home would have ruined her ultimate happiness—and her character. Mr. Burghersh would have forgiven her, and her fault—and it was a very grave one—would speedily have been forgotten by her ; she might even have hankered after that man again. And she wanted discipline. I never saw any one who wanted it worse ' (this made the Chief sit up with a vengeance) ' and those long months of suffering and repentance were absolutely necessary to effect a lasting change in her. The noble example of faith and endurance that her husband set her, and which won her deepest regard, would never have been afforded had she returned to him immediately after her mad caprice had stopped just short of actual wrong-doing, and *his* happiness would have been ruined in the end also.' Bully for Mater ! ' "

" But father has had a dreadful time," said

Nan, who positively exhaled happiness on the
frosty air, "and he's so good to me now,
again.   He knows I always stood up for
Easter, and what do you think he called me
this morning?—his—his 'clever little girl!'
And he always loved Basil to the very
bottom of his man's heart—and girls may
love *more*, but I think men love longest,
Daddy, and in a tougher sort of way—don't
you?"

Daddy nodded.   If *his* love had not been
pretty tough, it certainly never would have
stood the strain his idol put upon it.

"And I admire Jem's pluck in taking his
wife and the kid back to the Shaw," continued Daddy, who had taken up the chopper
and was whittling idly at the battered old
block, that in some grotesque way suggested
an ill-used but smiling countenance that
seemed to share in the general satisfaction.
"He won't even take the trouble to explain
that she's been at Minsterton every day of the

time since she left Penroses, and he's quite
right, explanations are odorous—and Jem
wisely avoids 'em. Neither he nor Easter
ever cared a hang for the county—though
that will be all right enough when it reads a
tit-bit in its to-day's *Times*," and he threw
down the chopper to fish a newspaper out of
his breast pocket, nodding meaningly as he
held it high out of Nan's reach. "Softly,"
he said, with an expression of great content,
" newspapers aren't fit readings for little
girls, you know—but nobody can say that
Easter was with Strokoff after *this* "—and he
rapped a particular column smartly—"because
he went straight from Penroses to town and
thence to Paris, and the rest of it, and his
travelling companion happened to have a
husband, you know—I mean," said Daddy
floundering, " that the husband had the bad
taste to make a row, and, in fact, he divorced
the lady, and here are all the dates and
everything, and a decree nisi—covers an

45*

awful lot that little word *nisi*, Nan! And
nobody can say anything worse of Easter than
that she took a drive at an unusual hour with
me—*me*, if you please, over to see mother—
and liked Minsterton, and mother, and me, so
much, she chose to stop there for a whole six
months, having got tired of the Shaw, the air
not exactly suiting her, and I shouldn't
wonder if *I* come out as the Don Juan of the
occasion, O ! *Lord !* "

" Yes, but there's the smudge, Daddy," said
Nan pitifully. " It's like some of mine that
won't rub out, however hard I try ! "

" Stuff ! " said Daddy, robustly, " the world
finds it morally impossible to quarrel with
twenty thousand a year, and the less
you want *it*, the more it wants *you*. The
whole thing will be forgotten in three
months—and if Easter will only take the
trouble to feed the brutes, they'll fawn
upon her ! "

Nan drew a long breath, and sat for a time

very quiet, with thinking eyes, and her thin hands folded in her lap.

"Daddy," she said at last very earnestly, and looking at his long Don Quixote-like countenance with eyes that blessed and caressed it, "it's you—just *you* who have brought it out all right for Easter—who have been a brick to her from first to last—who have made us all happy, and made the sun shine for us again, and I want to tell you, Daddy, that from the very bottom of my soul, I respect and *love* you!"

"Well, I'm blowed!" said Dinkie's outraged voice behind them, and Nan turned to behold her censor, who had secretly felt her defection very keenly, and greatly missed not only her company, but also having no one to lecture and improve "I wouldn't give myself away like that if I were you," and ignoring Daddy, he ostentatiously pretended to be looking for something hidden in a remote corner.

"No, you wouldn't, I daresay," said Nan with surprising tartness, " it isn't everybody who can *afford* to give himself away—there'd be nothing left—*I've* always got a large piece of myself left over, to do what I like with!"

Dinkie whistled. Nan was getting her head up again with a vengeance, and, for once he felt powerless to crush her, but Daddy laughed as he picked up his long limbs and made for the door. He applauded that instinct in Nan, bred by injustice, which bears a great deal, but at last rises, and calmly suppresses the oppressor.

"Good-bye, Nan," he said, " and thank you for saying you love me—it makes me proud. And you won't want me so often now, you know," and he glanced round with an odd feeling of affection at the homely walls as if they represented a part of his life. "Dear old hut," he said ; " you've put in some bad hours here, Nan, but you'll have lots of good ones yet. I shall come and look you up sometimes," and he nodded to her, and passed out.

Nan's face shadowed. Daddy had been a real comfort to her before she knew he had done anything for Easter, but now a sense of actual desolation overcame her, and turning up the skirt of her gown, she wept unrestrainedly behind it.

Dinkie's face twitched, and he made a half movement towards her, for at the bottom of his soul he was ashamed of his selfish behaviour about Easter, and secretly envied Nan, who had taken the right ground all through in the matter—as in spite of her faults he was beginning to see she nearly always did—in fact, in most things she was nearly as good as a *man*.

" There, don't cry," he said roughly, " all's well that ends well, you know. Easter's all right, and it's precious little besides her and your dear Daddy you care for nowadays. I might be dead for all *you'd* care."

Nan stopped crying gradually, and dried her eyes with a frayed piece of alpaca lining.

It was something for Dinkie even to notice her, for she would cheerfully endure his revilings rather than his silence any day, and a feeling of warmth stole through her heart.

"Daddy is *kind* to me," she said, and her tears rose again.

Dinkie looked sharply at her small face— much smaller and wanner surely than it used to be when he and she bickered amicably, week in, and week out, together, then crossed over, and gave her a rough hug.

"You know, Nan," he said half sheepishly, "that you like *me* best. Friends, eh?"

He produced two large Marie Louise pears, and gave her one. They sat down side by side on the faggots of wood to eat them, and peace, profound and all embracing, reigned in Nan's soul. Yet the child had taken her first long step out of childhood, and towards the self-assertiveness of the grown human ; the boy, his first painful one towards self-suppression, as they silently munched their fruit in the cold together.

CHAPTER VIII.

" Fresh perils past, fresh sins forgiven,
    New thoughts of God, new hopes of Heaven."

HUGON never gave to any living soul an account of her interview with Basil Strokoff when, having easily tracked him by the aid of a detective, and the clue of his own remarkable personality, she came up with him in St. Petersburgh.

It was characteristic of him to go where, at any moment, he might be conducted across the frontier, but he looked unconcerned and fresh as ever, with a volume of Pouschkine in his hand, when Hugon, travel-stained and disordered, feeling as though endless gates clashing behind her, had conducted her to a prison, whence all escape was cut off, suddenly appeared before him.

" Where is Easter ? " she said, glancing round the room, costly with exotics as are the dwellings of princes in that land of strangest and most violent contrasts.

" At the Shaw, I imagine," he said, looking at her with surprise, then struck by her expression, he added—" where else should she be ? "

Hugon crossed the salon, and opened the door into the third room forming his suite ; but, nest of luxury as the apartment was, she saw no sign of woman's occupation in it, and she came back to him, trembling.

" What have you done with her ? " she said. " You know that she is not at the Shaw. O ! my God ! have you deserted her already ? "

" I left her with Daddy Gardner," he said, his brow darkening at a recollection, for to receive two such checks as he had done, from so insignificant a person, infuriated him even to think of.

" And the woman you brought away with

you," stammered Hugon, too stunned to take in the full significance of what he said—" for it was not Mrs. Hoyos!"

Basil smiled slowly, and the smile was a revelation to her.

" Do you think there are only two women in a man's life?" he said. "And a man likes what he can *get*."

" Who was she—where is she?" cried Hugon, not daring to grasp all at once the great and glorious revelation that meant— what did it *not* mean to Jem?

" I sent her home yesterday," said Basil, languidly, and half closing his eyes as if to shut out a recollection of something that bored him. "Russia did not suit her constitution. Let me order some coffee for you," and he touched a bell.

" But—but," said Hugon, still, as it were, trickling her joy through her heart, lest she drowned in it, " you left Town for abroad a few hours after you arrived, and with a lady."

"Coffee," said Basil to the man who bowed before him. "It was very simple," he said when the door had closed, "I arrived at 7 a.m. bathed, breakfasted, sent my man round to a lady of my acquaintance with a note, telling him not to wait as there was no answer, caught the early train to Dover from Victoria —the lady was waiting for me at the latter place—and since then have been travelling. I did not see the necessity of writing home, the more especially as my father would object to my presence in Russia, where I have business. But why this chase? The virtuous Mrs. Burghersh is no doubt now quite happy in the arms of her *Jem*." He said the word savagely, and ground his heel into the rug at his feet. "So much impression I had made on her as that—*Jem* was scratched deep into her heart, and she did not know it. Well, I meant to read her a lesson, and I took her away more from pique and rage, than anything else—it was nearer revenge—for she had made a fool of me. I could have sworn she loved me—and all the while she kept control over herself, while I had none, and when she got away from me that night—it was her prattling of *Jem* did it—I swore a black oath that if she ever fell into my hands again, I would take her and break her, even if I sent her back the next day, I would break her, and punish her, for the way she had fooled me. And she played into my hands by trying to run away from me in the night. From something she let fall I guessed she meant to do it—I was in the garden and I followed, and caught her, and she might have come, though I believe she would have killed herself and me too first, but Nan——" he stopped abruptly, and a scarlet flush swept up to his brow, " dear Nan, brave Nan, who believed in me though I told her what I was, and am, tried to save us both, and I thrust her away—God forgive me, it was a cowardly blow ! "

He turned aside, and while his back was

turned to her, the coffee was brought in, and set before her.

"I always kept my bad manners for Penroses," he said, more quietly, presently. "Hound that I was, I behaved like a savage to her, but she never loved me, there was much pride and some feminine jealousy too in the matter, and she was not the woman to make me love her as I could love—and passion may grow out of love, but never love out of passion. And it was because I felt that I had behaved like a scoundrel and come with no good intentions to Penroses that when I heard of Mr. Denison's trouble, I assisted him —and so to some extent righted myself with my conscience. And but for you"—he added sternly, "you who threw us continually together—who moved heaven and earth to bring us into one another's arms—even produced those old letters of mine at a critical moment— damn them!" he interpolated heartily—"I wish my hand had rotted before it wrote

them, I should have done Easter no harm. I
don't know what your game was—possibly to
console *Jem* (his bitter accent showed that the
wound to his vanity still bled) but, however
you put it, you behaved about as badly and
treacherously as a woman can, to the people
who had benefited you."

Hugon seemed to shrivel as she stood
before her haughty accuser.

" It's all true," she said with difficulty, " but
I've repented . . . I'm trying to put it
all right again now . . . only *where* is
Easter ? Not at Penroses or the Hangingshaw ; no one has heard of her since you took
her away that night."

Basil started, and became very grave.

" What tricks has Gardner been up to ? "
he said, " it strikes me that young gentleman
is rather wasting his talents for intrigue in
the country. He drove off with her—or she
with him—and that was the last I saw of her.
Good God ! " he cried, as one struck by a

frightful thought, " do they think she is with *me*—do Denison and Nan think *that*?"

" How could they think any other? Have you not heard from your mother—it is with her money I have tracked you—from Mrs. Hoyos?"

Basil shook his head. He was very pale now, and his blue eyes looked black with suppressed emotion.

" Tell me," he said briefly, and she told him.

" That Denison should believe me to be such a sweep," he cried, forgetting what endeavours he had made to *be* one (it is always the sins that we have tried our hardest to commit, and been saved from, that we most resent being accused of). " That cuts the most of all—and with those business relations between us—why, he must have felt he'd *sold* her—and as to that Gardner " (he swore deep in his heart) " he ought to be boiled for muddling things so. It won't bear thinking

about.   I'll start for England at once," and
he tore at the bell, and desired Sanders to be
sent to him immediately.

The man came, as unruffled as when he had
put Lala Hoyos on a false scent before
leaving town to rejoin his master, but when
passports had been obtained, and everything
was prepared for the journey, Basil suddenly
decided to remain where he was.

Jem Burghersh was the proper person to
search for his wife, Basil could do little
good, but considerable harm, by appearing in
the neighbourhood, but this he could and
did do—write a letter to Tom Denison clearing
himself entirely of the odium that clung
about his name.   This letter, together with a
shorter one to Nan, Hugon took back to
England with her, but for reasons long ago
mentioned, they never reached the hands for
which they were intended, till Easter's child
was born, and all the truth made known.

*   *   *   *   *

Take one last journey with me before we part . . . step aside to where in a sunny corner of the little old-world churchyard into which Minsterton looks, Nan is tending the flowers she planted beside a grave at whose head is a slab of pure white marble, and upon which is cut in scarlet letters, the name :

HUGON.

Immediately below it is written "God be merciful to me, a Sinner."

*　　*　　*　　*　　*

Hither too, come Mrs. Gardner, and Daddy, even sometimes Dinkie, and there is innocent jest, and gentle fun and frolic, all that Nan thinks as suitable to death as life, above this woman who would have loved to know herself not forgotten, and hither, too, come Jem and beautiful Easter, with their little son who makes careful patterns of flowers, and prattles above the heart of the woman who loved his father truly, sinfully, but purely well at last.

It is here that Basil finds Nan the girl when
he comes to ask her forgiveness, here that
they talk hand in hand together, lovingly as
in former days, and hence that lingeringly
he passes out of her life for ever, *her* Basil,
and so leaves her comforted, not knowing
that on this earth their faces will never
quicken for joy at sight of each other
again, nor find in them a beauty that no
others see, but the man takes away with
him the one good, abiding woman-influence
that he has ever known in his life—and the
last.

For woman was nothing to Basil now—she
had been swept away like tow by sterner
thoughts, and the fierce breath of patriotism,
and Prince Strokoff saw, without blenching
for his only son, the approach of those perilous
years of struggle that might guide him to the
darkness of a Siberian mine, or on the other
hand throne him high among that brilliant list
of martyrs over whose lives their country has

advanced yet a few more blood-stained steps to freedom.

*   *   *   *   *

And as time went on, and Basil did not take his place with other marionettes on that ceaseless wheel of what they were pleased to call pleasure, Lala's smile grew rarer, and the small, pale face narrower and colder, while that infallible sign of corruption in a woman—the coarsening of her voice—began to betray her. She came to realize that love is the pivot upon which the merry-go-round of life turns, and when that pivot is worn out, or broken, the jocund figures fall lifeless from their seats ; there is no soul, or heart, or joyousness in the show—yea, the very music is dumb, and the dancing feet are stilled, when love himself is dead, or having gone out, hath forgotten to return.

THE END.

PRINTED BY
KELLY AND CO. LIMITED, 182, 183 AND 184 HIGH HOLBORN, W.C.,
AND KINGSTON-ON-THAMES.

14, Bedford Street, Strand,
London, **W.C.**

F. V. WHITE & CO.'S

LIST OF

PUBLICATIONS.

NEW
NOVELS AT ALL CIRCULATING LIBRARIES.

THE SOUL OF THE BISHOP.
By JOHN STRANGE WINTER, Author of "Bootles' Baby," "The Other Man's Wife," "Army Society," &c. 2 vols. (Second Edition.)

A MAN OF TO-DAY.
By HELEN MATHERS, Author of "Comin' thro' the Rye," "What the Glass Told," "T'other Dear Charmer," &c. 3 vols.

THE ENDING OF MY DAY; the Story of a Stormy Life.
By "RITA," Author of "The Man in Possession," "The Countess Pharamond," "The Laird o' Cockpen," &c. 3 vols.

A GREAT TEMPTATION.
By DORA RUSSELL, Author of "Footprints in the Snow," "Out of Eden," "The Last Signal," &c. 3 vols.

MY CHILD AND I. A Woman's Story.
By FLORENCE WARDEN, Author of "A Young Wife's Trial," "A Wild Wooing," "A Witch of the Hills," &c. 3 vols.

INTO TEMPTATION.
By A. PERRIN. 2 vols.

A BURIED SIN.
By the late Lady DUFFUS HARDY, Author of "Beryl Fortescue," "Paul Wynter's Sacrifice," "A Dangerous Experiment," &c. 3 vols.

A TRAGIC BLUNDER.
By MRS. LOVETT CAMERON, Author of "In a Grass Country," "Jack's Secret," "A Daughter's Heart," &c. 2 vols.

THE HAMPSTEAD MYSTERY.
By FLORENCE MARRYAT, Author of "My Sister the Actress," "Facing the Footlights," "The Heart of Jane Warner," &c. 3 vols.

THE HUNTING GIRL.
By MRS. EDWARD KENNARD, Author of "The Girl in the Brown Habit," "Wedded to Sport," "A Homburg Beauty," &c. 3 vols.

A THIRD PERSON.
By B. M. CROKER, Author of "Proper Pride," "Interference," "Two Masters," &c. 2 vols.

FOR ONE SEASON ONLY. A Sporting Novel.
By MRS. ROBERT JOCELYN, Author of "The M.F.H.'s Daughter," "Drawn Blank," &c. 3 vols.

UTTERLY MISTAKEN.
By ANNIE THOMAS (Mrs. PENDER CUDLIP), Author of "Allerton Towers," "Denis Donne," "Eyre of Blendon," &c. 3 vols.

A GIRL'S PAST.
By MRS. HERBERT MARTIN, Author of "Bonnie Lesley," "A Man and a Brother," "Common Clay," &c. 3 vols.

F. V. WHITE & Co., 14, Bedford Street, Strand.

THE WORKS OF JOHN STRANGE WINTER.

UNIFORM IN STYLE AND PRICE.

(At all Booksellers' and Bookstalls.)   In Paper Covers, 1/-; Cloth, 1/6 each.

A MAN'S MAN. (4th Edition.)

THAT MRS. SMITH. (2nd Edition.)

THREE GIRLS. (3rd Edition.)

MERE LUCK. (3rd Edition.)

LUMLEY THE PAINTER. (3rd Edition.)

GOOD-BYE. (7th Edition.)

HE WENT FOR A SOLDIER. (8th Edition.)

FERRERS COURT. (6th Edition.)

BUTTONS. (8th Edition.)

A LITTLE FOOL. (10th Edition.)

MY POOR DICK.
(10th Edition.) Illustrated by MAURICE GREIFFENHAGEN.

BOOTLES' CHILDREN.

(11th Edition.) Illustrated by J. BERNARD PARTRIDGE.
"John Strange Winter is never more thoroughly at home than when delineating the characters of children, and everyone will be delighted with the dignified Madge and the quaint Pearl. The book is mainly occupied with the love affairs of Terry (the soldier servant who appears in many of the preceding books), but the children buzz in and out of its pages much as they would come in and out of a room in real life, pervading and brightening the house in which they dwell."—*Leicester Daily Post.*

THE CONFESSIONS OF A PUBLISHER.

"The much discussed question of the relations between a publisher and his clients furnishes Mr. John Strange Winter with material for one of the brightest tales of the season. Abel Drinkwater's autobiography is written from a humorous point of view; yet here, as elsewhere, 'many a true word is spoken in jest,' and in the conversations of the publisher and his too ingenuous son facts come to light that are worthy of the attention of aspirants to literary fame."—*Morning Post.*

MIGNON'S HUSBAND. (14th Edition.)

"It is a capital love story, full of high spirits, and written in a dashing style that will charm the most melancholy of readers into hearty enjoyment of its fun."—*Scotsman.*

THAT IMP. (12th Edition.)

"Barrack life is abandoned for the nonce, and the author of 'Bootles' Baby' introduces readers to a country home replete with every comfort, and containing men and women whose acquaintanceship we can only regret can never blossom into friendship.'—*Whitehall Review.*
"This charming little book is bright and breezy, and has the ring of supreme truth about it."—*Vanity Fair.*

MIGNON'S SECRET. (17th Edition.)

"In 'Mignon's Secret' Mr. Winter has supplied a continuation to the never-to-be-forgotten 'Bootles' Baby.' . . . The story is gracefully and touchingly told."—*John Bull.*

F. V. WHITE & Co., 14, Bedford Street, Strand.

THE WORKS OF JOHN STRANGE WINTER—*(continued)*.

ON MARCH. (10th Edition.)

"This short story is characterised by Mr. Winter's customary truth in detail, humour, and pathos."—*Academy.*

"By publishing 'On March,' Mr J. S. Winter has added another little gem to his well-known store of regimental sketches. The story is written with humour and a deal of feeling."—*Army & Navy Gazette.*

IN QUARTERS. (11th Edition.)

"'In Quarters' is one of those rattling tales of soldiers' life which the public have learned to thoroughly appreciate."—*The Graphic.*

"The author of 'Bootles' Baby' gives us here another story of military life, which few have better described."—*British Quarterly Review.*

ARMY SOCIETY; Life in a Garrison Town.

Cloth, 6/-; Picture Boards, 2/-. (10th Edition.)

"This discursive story, dealing with life in a garrison town, is full of pleasant 'go' and movement which has distinguished 'Bootles' Baby,' 'Pluck,' or in fact a majority of some half-dozen novelettes which the author has submitted to the eyes of railway bookstall patronisers."—*Daily Telegraph.*

"The strength of the book lies in its sketches of life in a garrison town, which are undeniably clever. . . . It is pretty clear that Mr. Winter draws from life."—*St James's Gazette.*

GARRISON GOSSIP, Gathered in Blankhampton.

(A Sequel to "ARMY SOCIETY.") Cloth, 2/6; Picture Boards, 2/ (6th Edition.)

"'Garrison Gossip' may fairly rank with 'Cavalry Life,' and the various other books with which Mr. Winter has so agreeably beguiled our leisure hours."—*Saturday Review.*

"The novel fully maintains the reputation which its author has been fortunate enough to gain in a special line of his own."—*Graphic.*

A SIEGE BABY. Cloth, 2/6; Picture boards, 2/- (5th Edition.)

"The story which gives its title to this new sheaf of stories by the popular author of 'Bootles' Baby' is a very touching and pathetic one. . . . Amongst the other stories, the one entitled, 'Out of the Mists' is, perhaps, the best written, although the tale of true love it embodies comes to a most melancholy ending."—*County Gentleman.*

BEAUTIFUL JIM. (8th Edition.)

Cloth, 2/6; Picture Boards, 2/-

MRS. BOB. (7th Edition.)

Cloth, 2/6. Picture Boards, 2/-

THE OTHER MAN'S WIFE. (5th Edition.)

Cloth, 2/6. Picture Boards, 2/-

MY GEOFF; or, The Experiences of a Lady-Help. (6th Edition.) Cloth 2/6; Picture Boards, 2/-

ONLY HUMAN. (4th Edition). Cloth 2/6. Picture Boards, 2/-

AUNT JOHNNIE. (2nd Edition.) Cloth, 2/6

F. V. WHITE & Co., 14, Bedford Street, Strand.

NOVELS BY MRS. EDWARD KENNARD.

(At all Booksellers' and Bookstalls.)

JUST LIKE A WOMAN. (A New Novel.) Cloth gilt, 2s. 6d.

WEDDED TO SPORT. Cloth gilt, 3/6.

SPORTING TALES. (A New Work.) Cloth gilt, 2/6.

TWILIGHT TALES. (Illustrated.) Cloth gilt, 2/6. (2nd Edition.)

THAT PRETTY LITTLE HORSE-BREAKER.
(4th Edition.) Cloth gilt, 2s. 6d. Picture Boards, 2/-

A HOMBURG BEAUTY. (3rd Edition.) Cloth gilt, 2s. 6d.
Picture Boards, 2s.

MATRON OR MAID? (4th Edition.)
Cloth gilt, 2s. 6d. ; Picture Boards, 2s.

LANDING A PRIZE. (7th Edition.)
Cloth gilt, 2s. 6d. Picture Boards, 2/-

A CRACK COUNTY. (6th Edition.)
Cloth gilt, 2/6 ; Picture Boards, 2s.

THE GIRL IN THE BROWN HABIT.
Cloth gilt, 2/6 ; Picture Boards, 2/-. (8th Edition.)
" 'Nell Fitzgerald' is an irreproachable heroine, full of gentle womanliness, an i
rich in all virtues that make her kind estimable. Mrs. Kennard's work is marked
by high tone as well as vigorous narrative, and sportsmen, when searching for something new and beguiling for a wet day or spell of frost, can hardly light upon anything better than these fresh and picturesque hunting stories of Mrs. Kennard's."—
Daily Telegraph.

KILLED IN THE OPEN.
Cloth gilt, 2/6 ; Picture Boards, 2/-. (9th Edition.)
" It is in truth a very good love story set in a framework of hounds and horses,
but one that could be read with pleasure independently of any such attractions."—
Fortnightly Review.
" 'Killed in the Open ' is a very superior sort of hunting novel indeed,"—*Graphic.*

STRAIGHT AS A DIE.
Cloth gilt, 2/6 ; Picture Boards, 2/-. (9th Edition.)
" If you like sporting novels I can recommend to you Mrs. Kennard's 'Straight as
a Die,' "—*Truth.*

A REAL GOOD THING.
Cloth gilt, 2/6 ; Picture Boards, 2/-. (8th Edition.)
" There are some good country scenes and country spins in 'A Real Good Thing.
The hero, poor old Hopkins, is a strong character."—*Academy.*

OUR FRIENDS IN THE HUNTING-FIELD.
Cloth gilt, 2s. 6d. ; Picture Boards, 2s.

BY THE SAME AUTHOR.
In Paper Covers, 1/- ; Cloth, 1/6.

THE MYSTERY OF A WOMAN'S HEART.

F. V. WHITE & Co., 14, Bedford Street, Strand.

NOVELS BY HAWLEY SMART.

(At all Booksellers' & Bookstalls.)

BEATRICE AND BENEDICK: A Romance of the Crimea.
Cloth, 2/6 ; Picture Boards, 2/-. (2nd Edition.)
THE PLUNGER.
Cloth gilt, 2/6. Picture Boards, 2/-. (6th Edition.)
LONG ODDS.
Cloth gilt, 2/6. Picture Boards, 2/- (5th Edition.)
THE MASTER OF RATHKELLY.
Cloth gilt, 2/6. Picture Boards, 2/- (5th Edition.)
THE OUTSIDER.
Cloth gilt, 2/6. Picture Boards, 2/- (8th Edition.)

BY THE SAME AUTHOR. In Paper Covers, 1/-; Cloth, 1/6,
VANITY'S DAUGHTER.

NOVEL BY MRS. OLIPHANT.

THE SORCERESS. Cloth, 3/6.

NOVELS BY B. L. FARJEON.

(At all Booksellers' & Bookstalls.)
Cloth, 2/6. Picture Boards, 2/- each.
THE MARCH OF FATE. (Cloth only.)
BASIL AND ANNETTE. (2nd Edition.)
THE MYSTERY OF M. FELIX.
A YOUNG GIRL'S LIFE. (3rd Edition.)
TOILERS OF BABYLON. (2nd Edition.)
THE DUCHESS OF ROSEMARY LANE. (2nd Edition.)

In Paper Covers, 1/-; Cloth, 1/6 each.
A VERY YOUNG COUPLE.
THE PERIL OF RICHARD PARDON. (2nd Edition.)
A STRANGE ENCHANTMENT.

NOVELS BY B. M. CROKER.

(At all Booksellers' & Bookstalls.)
INTERFERENCE. (3rd Edition.) Cloth, 2/6; Picture Boards, 2/-.
TWO MASTERS. (3rd Edition.) Cloth, 2/6; Picture Boards, 2/-

NOVELS BY HELEN MATHERS.

(At all Booksellers' & Bookstalls.)
In Paper Covers, 1/-; Cloth, 1/6 each.
WHAT THE GLASS TOLD.
A STUDY OF A WOMAN, or VENUS VICTRIX.
T'OTHER DEAR CHARMER.
MY JO, JOHN. (2nd Edition.)
THE MYSTERY OF No. 13. (2nd Edition.)

SIR RANDAL H. ROBERTS, BART'S, SPORTING NOVELS
(At all Booksellers' and Bookstalls.)

NOT IN THE BETTING. (A New Novel.) Cloth gilt, 2/6.
CURB AND SNAFFLE. Cloth gilt, 2/6.

NOVELS BY MRS. ALEXANDER FRASER.
(At all Booksellers' and Bookstalls.)

A MODERN BRIDEGROOM. (2nd Edition.) Cloth, 2/6.
THE NEW DUCHESS. (2nd Edition.) Cloth, 2s. 6d.
DAUGHTERS OF BELGRAVIA. Cloth, 2/6. Also Picture Boards, 2/-
SHE CAME BETWEEN. Cloth, 2/6.

MRS. LOVETT CAMERON'S NOVELS.
(At all Booksellers' and Bookstalls.)

A SISTER'S SIN. Cloth, 2/6.
IN A GRASS COUNTRY.
    (A Story of Love and Sport.) (10th Edition.) Cloth gilt, 2/6; Picture
    Boards, 2/-; Paper Covers, 1/-.
    "We turn with pleasure to the green covers of 'In a Grass Country.' The three
heroines are charming each in her own way. It is well sketched, full of character,
with sharp observations of men and women—not too hard on anybody—a clear story
carefully written, and therefore easily read. . . . recommended."—*Punch.*
    "When the days are short and there is an hour or two to be disposed of indoors
before dressing time, one is glad to be able to recommend a good and amusing novel.
'In a Grass Country' may be said to come under this description."—*Saturday
Review.*
WEAK WOMAN. (3rd Edition.) Cloth 2/6. Picture Boards, 2/-.
JACK'S SECRET. (3rd Edition.) Cloth, 2/6. Picture Boards, 2/-
A LOST WIFE. (3rd Edition.) Cloth, 2/6. Picture Boards, 2/-
A DAUGHTER'S HEART. Cloth, 2s. 6d.

BY

JUSTIN M'CARTHY, M.P.
AND
MRS. CAMPBELL PRAED.
(Authors of "The Right Honourable," &c.)
(At all Booksellers' and Bookstalls.)

THE LADIES' GALLERY.
    (2nd Edition.) Cloth, 2/6; Picture Boards, 2/-.
THE RIVAL PRINCESS; a London Romance of To-day.
    (3rd Edition.) Cloth, 2s. 6d.; Picture Boards, 2s.

BY MRS. CAMPBELL PRAED.
(At all Booksellers' and Bookstalls.)
THE ROMANCE OF A CHÂLET. (Cloth 2/6.)

BY MRS. J. H. RIDDELL.
A SILENT TRAGEDY. Paper Covers, 1/-; Cloth, 1/6.

F. V. WHITE & Co., 14, Bedford Street, Strand.

MRS. ALEXANDER'S NOVELS.
(At all Booksellers' and Bookstalls.)

FOUND WANTING. Cloth, 2s. 6d.
FOR HIS SAKE. Cloth, 2/6.
A WOMAN'S HEART. Cloth, 2/6.
BLIND FATE. Cloth, 2/6; Picture Boards, 2/-.
BY WOMAN'S WIT. (6th Edition.) Picture Boards, 2/-;
Cloth, 2/6.

> " In Mrs. Alexander's tale
> Much art she clearly shows
> In keeping dark the mystery
> Until the story's close."—*Punch.*

WELL WON. Cloth, 1s. 6d. only.

NOVELS BY HUME NISBET.
(At all Booksellers' and Bookstalls.)

A BUSH-GIRL'S ROMANCE. With Illustrations by the
Author. Cloth, 3/6.
THE HAUNTED STATION and other Stories. With
Illustrations by the Author. Cloth gilt, 2/6.
THE QUEEN'S DESIRE ; A Romance of the Indian Mutiny.
Cloth, 3s. 6d. (Illustrated) ; Picture Boards, 2s.
THE BUSHRANGER'S SWEETHEART ; An Australian
Romance. Cloth, 2/6 ; Picture Boards, 2/-. (5th Edition.)
THE SAVAGE QUEEN ; A Romance of the Natives of Van
Dieman's Land. Cloth, 2/6 ; Picture Boards, 2/-. (3rd Edition.)

"RITA'S" NOVELS.
(AT ALL BOOKSELLERS' AND BOOKSTALLS.)

SHEBA : A Study of Girlhood. (4th Edition.) Cloth, 2s. 6d. ;
Picture Boards, 2/-.
THE COUNTESS PHARAMOND : A Sequel to "Sheba."
Cloth, 2/6.
THE MAN IN POSSESSION. (A New Novel.) Cloth, 2/6.
THE LAIRD O' COCKPEN. Cloth, 2/6.
MISS KATE. (4th Edition.) Cloth, 2/6 ; Picture Boards, 2/.
THE SEVENTH DREAM. 1/- and 1/6.
THE DOCTOR'S SECRET. (2nd Edition.) 1/- and 1/6.

AMYE READE'S WORK.
(At all Booksellers' and Bookstalls.)

SLAVES OF THE SAWDUST ; A New and Original Story of
Acrobat Life. By the Author of "Ruby," &c. Picture Boards, 2/-. Also
Cloth, 2/6. (Dedicated to the late Lord Tennyson.)

F. V. WHITE & Co., 14, Bedford Street, Strand.

ONE VOLUME NOVELS
BY POPULAR AUTHORS.

Crown 8vo., Cloth, 2s. 6d. each.

(AT ALL BOOKSELLERS' AND BOOKSTALLS.)

By JOHN STRANGE WINTER.

AUNT JOHNNIE.	MRS. BOB.
ONLY HUMAN.	BEAUTIFUL JIM.
MY GEOFF.	A SIEGE BABY.
THE OTHER MAN'S WIFE.	GARRISON GOSSIP.

By MRS. EDWARD KENNARD.

JUST LIKE A WOMAN. (A New Novel.)
WEDDED TO SPORT (3/6).
SPORTING TALES. (A New Work) | TWILIGHT TALES.
THAT PRETTY LITTLE HORSE-BREAKER.

A HOMBURG BEAUTY.	A CRACK COUNTY.
MATRON OR MAID?	A REAL GOOD THING.
LANDING A PRIZE.	STRAIGHT AS A DIE.

THE GIRL IN THE BROWN HABIT.
KILLED IN THE OPEN.
OUR FRIENDS IN THE HUNTING-FIELD.

By HAWLEY SMART.

BEATRICE AND BENEDICK.	THE PLUNGER.
THE MASTER OF RATHKELLY.	LONG ODDS.
THE OUTSIDER.	

By MRS. CAMPBELL PRAED.

THE ROMANCE OF A CHÂLET.

By B. L. FARJEON.

THE MYSTERY OF M. FELIX.	A YOUNG GIRL'S LIFE.
THE MARCH OF FATE.	BASIL AND ANNETTE.

TOILERS OF BABYLON.
THE DUCHESS OF ROSEMARY LANE.

By MAY CROMMELIN.

THE FREAKS OF LADY FORTUNE.

By FLORENCE WARDEN.

A YOUNG WIFE'S TRIAL; or Ralph Ryder of Brent.
A WITCH OF THE HILLS.
A WILD WOOING. (A New Novel.)

By MABEL COLLINS.	By Mrs. OLIPHANT.
VIOLA FANSHAWE.	THE SORCERESS (3/6).

By B. M. CROKER.

TWO MASTERS.	INTERFERENCE.

By HUME NISBET.

A BUSH GIRL'S ROMANCE (3/6.)
THE HAUNTED STATION and other Stories.
THE QUEEN'S DESIRE (Cloth, 3/6).
THE SAVAGE QUEEN.
THE BUSHRANGER'S SWEETHEART.

F. V. WHITE & Co., 14, Bedford Street, Strand.

ONE VOLUME NOVELS—*(continued)*.

By SIR RANDAL H. ROBERTS, Bart.
NOT IN THE BETTING. (A New Novel.)
CURB AND SNAFFLE.

By AMYE READE, (Author of "RUBY," &c.)
SLAVES OF THE SAWDUST.

By F. C. PHILIPS & C. J. WILLS.
SYBIL ROSS'S MARRIAGE.

By MRS. ALEXANDER.
FOUND WANTING.

BLIND FATE.	BY WOMAN'S WIT.
A WOMAN'S HEART.	FOR HIS SAKE.

By MRS. LOVETT CAMERON

A SISTER'S SIN.	A LOST WIFE.
IN A GRASS COUNTRY.	A DAUGHTER'S HEART.
JACK'S SECRET.	WEAK WOMAN.

By JUSTIN M'CARTHY, M.P. & Mrs. CAMPBELL PRAED.

THE RIVAL PRINCESS.	THE LADIES' GALLERY.

By MRS. ROBERT JOCELYN.

THE M.F.H.'s DAUGHTER.	DRAWN BLANK.
THE CRITON HUNT MYSTERY.	A BIG STAKE.
ONLY A HORSE-DEALER.	

By BRET HARTE.
THE CRUSADE OF THE "EXCELSIOR."

By the Honble. MRS. FETHERSTONHAUGH.
DREAM FACES.

By FERGUS HUME.
WHOM GOD HATH JOINED.
THE MAN WITH A SECRET.

By Mrs. HUNGERFORD, (Author of "MOLLY BAWN.")
THE HONBLE. MRS. VEREKER.

APRIL'S LADY.	LADY PATTY.
AN UNSATISFACTORY LOVER. (A New Novel).	

By "RITA."
THE COUNTESS PHARAMOND. A Sequel to "SHEBA."

THE MAN IN POSSESSION (A New Novel).	MISS KÂTE.
	THE LAIRD O' COCKPEN.
	SHEBA.

By MRS. ALEXANDER FRASER.

A MODERN BRIDEGROOM.	SHE CAME BETWEEN.
DAUGHTERS OF BELGRAVIA.	THE NEW DUCHESS.

By FLORENCE MARRYAT.
MY SISTER THE ACTRESS.

By MAY CROMMELIN and J. MORAY BROWN.
VIOLET VYVIAN, M.F.H.

By F. C. PHILIPS and PERCY FENDALL.
A DAUGHTER'S SACRIFICE.
MARGARET BYNG.
MY FACE IS MY FORTUNE.

POPULAR NOVELS.

Picture Boards, 2s. each.

(AT ALL BOOKSELLERS' AND BOOKSTALLS.)

ONLY HUMAN. (4th Edition.) By JOHN STRANGE WINTER.
MY GEOFF. (6th Edition.) By the same Author.
THE OTHER MAN'S WIFE. (5th Edition.) By the same Author.
MRS. BOB. (7th Edition.) By the same Author.
BEAUTIFUL JIM. (8th Edition.) By the same Author.
A SIEGE BABY. (5th Edition.) By the same Author.
GARRISON GOSSIP. (6th Edition.) By the same Author.
ARMY SOCIETY: Life in a Garrison Town. (10th Edition.) By
the same Author.
THE MAN WITH A SECRET. (3rd Edition.) By FERGUS HUME.
LONG ODDS. (5th Edition.) By HAWLEY SMART.
THE PLUNGER. (6th Edition.) By the same Author.
THE MASTER OF RATHKELLY. (5th Edition.) By the same
Author.
BEATRICE AND BENEDICK. (2nd Edition.) By the same Author.
THE OUTSIDER. (8th Edition.) By the same Author.
A LOST WIFE. (3rd Edition.) By Mrs. LOVETT CAMERON.
WEAK WOMAN. (3rd Edition.) By the same Author.
IN A GRASS COUNTRY. (10th Edition.) By the same Author.
JACK'S SECRET. (3rd Edition.) By the same Author.
BLIND FATE. By Mrs. ALEXANDER.
BY WOMAN'S WIT. (6th Edition.) By the same Author.
THE HON. MRS. VEREKER. (4th Edition.) By Mrs. HUNGERFORD,
Author of "Molly Bawn."
LADY PATTY. (3rd Edition.) By the same Author.
APRIL'S LADY. (4th Edition.) By the same Author.
LANDING A PRIZE. (7th Edition.) By Mrs. EDWARD KENNARD.
THAT PRETTY LITTLE HORSE-BREAKER. (4th Edition.)
By the same Author.
A HOMBURG BEAUTY. (3rd Edition.) By the same Author.
MATRON OR MAID? (4th Edition.) By the same Author.
A CRACK COUNTY. (6th Edition.) By the same Author.
A REAL GOOD THING. (8th Edition.) By the same Author.
STRAIGHT AS A DIE. (9th Edition.) By the same Author.
THE GIRL IN THE BROWN HABIT. (8th Edition.) By the
same Author.
OUR FRIENDS IN THE HUNTING-FIELD. By the same Author.
KILLED IN THE OPEN. (9th Edition.) By the same Author.

POPULAR   NOVELS—*(continued)*.

INTERFERENCE. (3rd Edition.) By B. M. CROKER.
TWO MASTERS. (3rd Edition.) By the same Author.
MISS KATE; or, Confessions of a Caretaker. (4th Edition.) By
   "RITA."
SHEBA: A Study of Girlhood. (4th Edition.) By the same
   Author.
TOILERS OF BABYLON. (2nd Edition.) By B. L. FARJEON.
THE DUCHESS OF ROSEMARY LANE. (2nd Edition.) By the
   same Author.
THE MYSTERY OF M. FELIX. By the same Author.
A YOUNG GIRL'S LIFE. (3rd Edition.) By the same Author.
BASIL AND ANNETTE. (2nd Edition.) By the same Author.
THE RIVAL PRINCESS. (3rd Edition.) By JUSTIN MCCARTHY,
   M.P., and Mrs. CAMPBELL PRAED.
THE LADIES' GALLERY. (2nd Edition.) By the same Authors.
A WOMAN'S FACE. By FLORENCE WARDEN, Author of "The
   House on the Marsh," &c.
A WILD WOOING. By the same Author.
A WITCH OF THE HILLS. (3rd Edition.) By the same Author.
VIOLET VYVIAN, M.F.H. (3rd Edition.) By MAY CROMMELIN
   and J. MORAY BROWN.
THE FREAKS OF LADY FORTUNE. By MAY CROMMELIN.
DAUGHTERS OF BELGRAVIA. By Mrs. ALEXANDER FRASER.
SYBIL ROSS'S MARRIAGE: The Romance of an Inexperienced
   Girl. (3rd Edition.) By F. C. PHILIPS and C. J. WILLS.
A DAUGHTER'S SACRIFICE. (3rd Edition.) By F. C. PHILIPS
   and PERCY FENDALL.
MARGARET BYNG. By the same Authors.
THE HEART OF JANE WARNER. By FLORENCE MARRYAT.
MY SISTER THE ACTRESS. By the same Author.
UNDER THE LILIES AND ROSES. By the same Author.
KATE VALLIANT. By ANNIE THOMAS (MRS. PENDER CUDLIP).
MATED WITH A CLOWN. By LADY CONSTANCE HOWARD.
KEITH'S WIFE. By LADY VIOLET GREVILLE.
THE CRUSADE OF THE "EXCELSIOR." By BRET HARTE.
SLAVES OF THE SAWDUST. (An Original Work.) By AMYE
   READE, Author of "Ruby."
NOT EASILY JEALOUS. By IZA DUFFUS HARDY.
ONLY A LOVE STORY. By the same Author.
POISONED ARROWS. By JEAN MIDDLEMASS.
THE SAVAGE QUEEN: A Romance of the Natives of Van
   Dieman's Land. (3rd Edition.) By HUME NISBET.
THE QUEEN'S DESIRE. A Romance of the Indian Mutiny. By
   the same Author.
THE BUSHRANGER'S SWEETHEART. An Australian Romance.
   (5th Edition.) By the same Author.
THE M.F.H.'s DAUGHTER. By Mrs. ROBERT JOCELYN.
THE CRITON HUNT MYSTERY. By the same Author.

ONE SHILLING NOVELS.

In Paper Covers.   (Cloth, 1s. 6d.)

(At all Booksellers' and Bookstalls.)

A MAN'S MAN. By JOHN STRANGE WINTER, Author of "Bootles' Baby," &c. (4th Edition.)

THAT MRS. SMITH. (2nd Edition.) By the same Author.

THREE GIRLS. (3rd Edition.) By the same Author.

MERE LUCK. (3rd Edition.) By the same Author.

LUMLEY THE PAINTER. (3rd Edition.) By the same Author.

GOOD-BYE. (7th Edition.) By the same Author.

HE WENT FOR A SOLDIER. (8th Edition.) By the same Author.

FERRERS COURT. (6th Edition.) By the same Author.

BUTTONS. (8th Edition.) By the same Author.

A LITTLE FOOL. (10th Edition.) By the same Author.

MY POOR DICK. (Illustrated by MAURICE GREIFFEN-HAGEN.) (10th Edition.) By the same Author.

BOOTLES' CHILDREN. (Illustrated by J. BERNARD PARTRIDGE.) (11th Edition.) By the same Author.

THE CONFESSIONS OF A PUBLISHER. By the same Author.

MIGNON'S HUSBAND. (14th Edition.) By the same Author.

THAT IMP. (12th Edition.) By the same Author.

MIGNON'S SECRET. (17th Edition.) By the same Author.

ON MARCH. (10th Edition.) By the same Author.

IN QUARTERS. (11th Edition.) By the same Author.

THE GENTLEMAN WHO VANISHED. (2nd Edition.) By FERGUS HUME.

THE PICCADILLY PUZZLE. By the same Author.

THE POWER OF AN EYE. By Mrs. FRANK ST. CLAIR GRIMWOOD, Author of "My Three Years in Manipur."

A VERY YOUNG COUPLE. By B. L. FARJEON, Author of "Toilers of Babylon," &c.

ONE SHILLING NOVELS—*(continued)*.

THE PERIL OF RICHARD PARDON. (2nd Edition.) By B. L. Farjeon.

A STRANGE ENCHANTMENT. By the same Author.

A SILENT TRAGEDY. By Mrs. J. H. Riddell, Author of " George Geith of Fen Court," &c.

THE MYSTERY OF No. 13. (2nd Edition.) By Helen Mathers, Author of " Comin' Thro' the Rye," &c.

WHAT THE GLASS TOLD. By the same Author.

A STUDY OF A WOMAN ; or, Venus Victrix. By the same Author.

MY JO, JOHN. (2nd Edition.) By the same Author.

T' OTHER DEAR CHARMER. By the same Author.

WELL WON. By Mrs. Alexander. (Cloth, only.)

TOM'S WIFE. By Lady Margaret Majendie, Author of " Fascination," " Sisters-in-Law," &c.

THE CONFESSIONS OF A DOOR MAT. By Alfred C. Calmour, Author of " The Amber Heart," &c.

THE MYSTERY OF A WOMAN'S HEART. By Mrs. Edward Kennard.

IN A GRASS COUNTRY. By Mrs. Lovett Cameron. (9th Edition.)

CITY AND SUBURBAN. (2nd Edition.) By Florence Warden, Author of " " The House on the Marsh," &c.

GRAVE LADY JANE. By the same Author.

A SHOCK TO SOCIETY. By the same Author.

THE DOCTOR'S SECRET. (2nd Edition.) By " Rita," Author of " Dame Durden," " Sheba," &c.

THE SEVENTH DREAM. By the same Author.

VANITY'S DAUGHTER. By Hawley Smart.

A CONQUERING HEROINE. By Mrs. Hungerford, Author of " Molly Bawn," &c.

A MAD PRANK. By the same Author.

A FRENCH MARRIAGE. By F. C. Philips.

FACING THE FOOTLIGHTS. By Florence Marryat.

PRICE ONE SHILLING.

BELGRAVIA:
A LONDON MAGAZINE.

(ESTABLISHED 1866.)

Terms of Subscription: Payable in advance.

TWELVE MONTHS (POST FREE) .. .. .. **12s.**
**DO.   INCLUDING THE SUMMER NUMBER
        AND CHRISTMAS ANNUAL** .. .. **14s.**

Elegantly Bound Volumes of "Belgravia," with Gilt Edges
(560 pages), price, 7/6 each. Vol. LXXXII. is now Ready.

(Cases for binding volumes, 2s. each.)

(AT ALL BOOKSELLERS' AND BOOKSTALLS.)

" 'Belgravia' begins the year with a remarkable advance both in its literature
and general 'get up,' and gives promise of the well-deserved return of its old
popularity."—*Life.*

" 'Belgravia' is one of the most thoroughly entertaining of all the monthlies
which supply their readers with the lighter forms of literature. Its fiction is of a
high order, and its shorter sketches and stories are little gems in their way, with
scarcely a dull page in the whole of them."—*North British Daily Mail.*

" 'Belgravia' keeps up the character for originality which it has held so long."—
Blackburn Times.

All Communications to be addressed to

THE EDITOR OF "BELGRAVIA,"
C/o F. V. WHITE & CO., 14, Bedford St., Strand, W.C.

PRICE ONE SHILLING.

LONDON SOCIETY.

(ESTABLISHED 1862.)

A MONTHLY MAGAZINE

Of Light and Amusing Literature by the most popular Authors of the day.

Terms of Subscription: Payable in advance.

TWELVE MONTHS (POST FREE) .. .. **12s.**
**DO.   INCLUDING THE SUMMER NUMBER
        AND THE CHRISTMAS NUMBER** .. **14s.**

Handsomely Bound Volumes of "London Society," each with a
Gilt Edge (780 pages), price, 10/6. Vol. LXIV. is now Ready.

(Cases for binding volumes, 2s. each.)

(AT ALL BOOKSELLERS' AND BOOKSTALLS.)

OPINIONS OF THE PRESS.

"Readers who like to be amused should take in 'London Society.' . . 'London
Society' is a good shillingsworth."—*Lady's Pictorial.*

"This attractive magazine is remarkable for variety of subject and excellence of
its light literature."—*Public Opinion.*

"Full of the light and amusing literature it professes to supply."—*Literary World.*

"It is bright, interesting, and a perfect mine of light and amusing literature. It is
ably conducted, and should enjoy an ever-increasing circulation."—*Grantham Times*

All communications to be addressed to

THE EDITOR OF "LONDON SOCIETY."
C/o F. V. WHITE & CO., 14, Bedford St., Strand, W.C.